"We're working together. No more going off on your own." Laurel tapped a finger against Mace's chest. **"Got it?"**

Mace caught her hand, stilled it. "What I do on my own time is my business."

A zing of awareness raced up her arm. "You and I are joined at the hip until we figure this thing out."

"You're a hard lady."

"No harder than I have to be."

He nudged her to the truck. "I want you off the streets. Don't forget, the Collective has put a bounty on you."

Laurel snorted. "And here we go again, back to where we started. I'm sticking with you. Get used to it."

Laurel didn't hear Mace's response—the rapid report of M4s reverberated through the night. The hiss of a bullet between her and Mace was too close for comfort. It buried itself into the dashboard.

"Stay down." Mace was already reaching for his Glock.

But Laurel didn't bother responding. She drew her weapon and opened the door.

Jane M. Choate dreamed of writing from the time she was a small child when she entertained friends with outlandish stories complete with happily-ever-after endings. Writing for Love Inspired Suspense is a dream come true. Jane is the proud mother of five children, grandmother to seven grandchildren and staff to one cat who believes she is of royal descent.

Books by Jane M. Choate

Love Inspired Suspense

Keeping Watch
The Littlest Witness
Shattered Secrets
High-Risk Investigation
Inherited Threat

INHERITED THREAT

JANE M. CHOATE

HARLEQUIN® LOVE INSPIRED® SUSPENSE

Recycling programs for this product may not exist in your area.

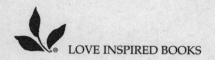 LOVE INSPIRED BOOKS

ISBN-13: 978-1-335-67910-9

Inherited Threat

www.Harlequin.com

Printed in U.S.A.

If God be for us, who can be against us?
—*Romans* 8:31

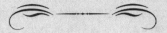

Dedicated to America's unsung heroes: military dogs. Military dogs save lives, sometimes at the expense of their own. These courageous animals provide comfort and companionship to American troops, detect explosive devices and even shield soldiers from flying bullets. A military dog was deployed by navy SEALs in the mission to capture Osama bin Laden. In 2009, a Silver Star, one of the navy's highest awards, was awarded posthumously to a dog named Remco after he charged an insurgent's hideout in Afghanistan.

ONE

The caw of a crow reverberated through the early morning air, scraping already frayed nerves. Senses spiking, Laurel Landry approached Bernice's—she had never earned the title *mother*—storage unit. Bernice's murder a week ago had brought Laurel to this shabby place at this moment.

Using the key she'd discovered in Bernice's ancient double-wide trailer, Laurel let herself in and began her search. Sammy, her German shepherd, stood guard.

Buried beneath a stack of boxes, she found a familiar "go-bag." From the time Laurel had been a small child, Bernice had kept a suitcase for when the two of them had to leave town in a hurry, usually just before the rent was due.

Inside the bag were three items: an envelope containing a picture of a lanky boy and a little girl that was labeled *Jake and Shelley* and dated more than twenty years ago, another photo, this one of Laurel's mother and bearing the same date, along with a newspaper article about S&J Security/Protection; a ledger with what might have been names and dates written in some kind of code, the word *Collective* on the front; and packets of hundred dollar bills. A quick estimate put the amount at ten thousand dollars.

Laurel stuffed the contents into her pack. The shiver that skittered down her spine had nothing to do with the chill of the cold locker and everything to do with the single word *Collective*.

What was Bernice doing with a ledger bearing the name of a group of organized crime families that had infiltrated public and private sectors from banking to the US Attorney's Office? News of the group's exploits had reached her even during deployment in the Middle East.

Bernice, what had you gotten yourself into?

Laurel shook her head, the action one of resignation rather than denial. She'd long ago accepted that Bernice never thought through a decision and that she rarely, if ever, considered the effect her actions might have on others, especially her daughter. Her involvement with the Collective was but one more in an increasingly long string of bad choices. There'd be no more bad choices on Bernice's part, Laurel reflected.

Though the Collective was based in Atlanta, its tentacles were everywhere, apparently even here in this speck of a town where Bernice had lived.

A chuff of noise outside the unit caused Laurel to go still. Had she been followed to the storage lockers? She'd been careful, but she had to admit that she had been more intent on reaching her destination than checking the rearview mirror.

Awareness feathered her senses. A tingle of apprehension raced through her. Ranger training had taught her to trust her instincts.

"Sammy," she whispered to her dog as she pulled on her backpack, "time to go."

Something in her voice must have alerted him for he went on point.

As she exited the unit, a large man swiped at her backpack. Fortunately, she had it secured around her waist as well as her shoulders.

"Oh, no, you don't," she yelled and jerked away from him.

He broadened his stance, the menacing move designed to intimidate. Too bad. She didn't scare. "Give me what I want, and you can go."

Like she believed that. "I don't have anything."

He ignored that and reached for her again.

Sammy growled menacingly but remained still. He was too well-trained to attack without a command from her.

Laurel knew she could take down the intruder. Ranger training had honed the already formidable skills she'd earned courtesy of the US Army. She twisted out of his reach and spun, kicking with her right leg and catching him in the chest cavity. The grunt of pain told her she'd made serious contact. *Good.*

He went down. Hard.

"Sammy, now."

Despite having only three legs, Sammy attacked, fastening his jaw around the man's ankle.

The man yelped. "Get him off me."

"Sammy, enough."

Sammy released his hold on the man.

She glared at her would-be assailant. "Stay still or you'll see what he can really do."

While he figured out that he wasn't getting away, Laurel did some thinking of her own. If she waited for the police, she'd be letting herself in for prolonged questioning. It didn't take much to surmise that the man belonged to the Collective and wanted the money and the ledger. Though she didn't understand the meaning of the coded numbers listed in it, she knew instinctively she couldn't let him have it.

Laurel pulled her weapon and held it on the man. "Sammy, watch."

With her other hand, she fished through his pockets, found a pair of handcuffs—had he planned on using them on her?—and a set of keys. When she pressed the key fob, a beep from a nearby truck identified it as his. She marched him to the vehicle.

"Open the driver's and back doors, then put the right cuff on." After he did so, she slipped the empty cuff through the exposed frame, clicked the second manacle around his other wrist and secured him there.

He struggled against the restraint, all the while spewing a stream of venom. Mean eyes glittered with hate. "This ain't over."

"You're right. It ain't. But you are."

The brief exchange sent her thoughts in a different direction. What if her career with the Rangers was over as a result of the injury she'd sustained while deployed?

She'd meticulously constructed her life, a result of her chaotic childhood. A need to put order to everything had driven her first to the Army, then the Rangers. There, she'd found the first real home she'd ever known. Being part of something bigger than herself gave her life purpose.

If she couldn't be a Ranger any longer, she feared her life would lose its meaning.

Nothing she could do about it now. At the moment, she was running for her life. There'd be time enough to worry over the future.

Whispers of pink streaked the sky as she headed out of town on a narrow road of chewed-up asphalt. She put a call in to the local police, gave the location of the storage unit and reported the man as a burglar.

Outside one of the small towns that dotted the backwoods road, she found a coffee shop that advertised free Wi-Fi. Though she was anxious to be on her way, she booted up her laptop. First, she contacted a friend at the DOJ and asked for any information he had on the Collective.

His answer came swiftly. Stay out of their way.

She typed back. Too late.

Okay, but you asked for it.

Page after page of text filled her screen. She dug out a thumb drive and copied the information to it.

Next she ran a search on S&J Security/Protection of Atlanta, Georgia. Articles about the firm were abundant, as were mentions of Jake Rabb and Shelley Rabb Judd and their emphasis on hiring ex-military and police personnel as operatives.

Laurel did some quick calculations in her head, taking in the date on the picture and the probable current ages of the Rabb brother and sister. Could it be? Did she have a half-brother and half-sister?

The idea filled her with such longing that tears stung her eyes. In the lonely years growing up, she'd prayed for a sister or brother, someone to laugh with, to cry with. The possibility that she had both a brother and a sister revived that childhood dream. If only…

She put away the wishful thinking and turned her attention to the practical. She was going to have to do something she hated, something that stuck in her craw like having to bow and scrape to a smarmy politician: she was going to have to ask for help. She texted the contact number for S&J Security/Protection, gave a bullet point explanation of her situation, adding that she was a Ranger in the States on medical leave. When a reply came within minutes saying that an S&J operative, an ex-Ranger no less, would meet her, she knew she was on the right track.

With a to-go mug of coffee and a bottle of water for Sammy's bowl, Laurel left the shop and started on her way once more. The road climbed, an easy ascent until it reached the ridge. From there, the ribbon of asphalt narrowed, twisting and looping back and forth on itself like a sidewinder as it gradually descended.

As she rounded the curves, she thought she caught a glimpse of headlights in her rearview mirror. When the pinpricks of light didn't appear again, she returned her focus to hugging the centerline of the road. Relief sighed through her when she reached the base of the valley and the road straightened out once more.

The breath caught in her throat when she noticed a jacked-up truck with oversize wheels following close behind.

Looked like she'd picked up a tail. The truck closed the distance between them until it was riding her bumper. Hard.

Laurel refused to give way to the truck that was trying to run her off the road. She made out two men. If she let them send her into the ditch, she'd be at a distinct disadvantage. A grim smile touched her lips at the understatement.

Rule one in combat: keep the upper hand.

"Hold on, Sammy."

The German shepherd, who rode shotgun, woofed in response.

She swerved, cutting off the truck's attempt to come up on her right side.

Despite its battered appearance, the truck had muscle behind it, and she had combat driving training on her side. She called upon every skill she had and slammed down the accelerator, rocketing ahead. She stepped on the gas and didn't let up. As the speed increased, her breathing slowed, steadied.

When she spotted a rutted road up ahead, nearly hidden by underbrush, she turned sharply, then held her breath when the truck passed in a tail of battered air and a boil of dust.

She wasn't one to waste time on self-congratulations, but she couldn't hold back a fist pump in the air followed by a brief prayer of gratitude. A scripture flashed into her mind. *If God be for us, who can be against us?*

Then it was back to business. The men would be back. What's more, they undoubtedly had others in their network who would be coming after her as well. She was outmanned and outgunned.

Laurel didn't run from trouble—Rangers typically ran toward it—but she wasn't foolhardy. Admitting that she needed help hadn't been easy, but she was grateful that an S&J operative was on his way. She only hoped he arrived in time.

Mace Ransom nosed into a parking spot at the mom-and-pop grocery store and waited for the client to show up. He climbed out of the truck and leaned against the fender. Anticipation sent adrenaline pumping through him as he replayed his boss's words in his mind.

We've got a new client who's found herself on the wrong side of the Collective. Laurel Landry. She needs backup, and she needs it now. Shelley Rabb Judd, founder and co-owner of S&J Security/Protection, had rattled off a name and directions to the meeting spot. *By the way, she's a Ranger, on medical leave.*

He had kitted up, including flexi-cuffs, flash bangs and a few other goodies, such as an H&K UMP, suppressed and chambered, along with his NVGs. His night vision goggles had come in handy on more than one occasion.

The Glock 17, his preferred weapon, he placed in a custom-made shoulder holster. All that was left was his K-bar knife, which he slid inside his boot. He traveled light and liked it that way. Too many possessions, too many emotions, slowed you down.

There'd been no one to contact, no one to let

know that he was going out of town. He supposed he ought to be grateful for the freedom.
Instead, it only emphasized the fact that he was
alone.

The spurt of self-pity annoyed him, and he
shoved aside the unaccustomed feelings to focus
on the job.

A battered sedan pulled in and a tall woman
climbed out, accompanied by a dog. She raked
Mace with a long look, then nodded, apparently
satisfied, and strode toward him.

"You're S&J, right?"

"Mace Ransom." He drew in a sharp breath,
not expecting the kick-to-the-gut attraction to
the lady. Beautiful didn't begin to describe her.

She was a job. He'd do well to remember that.

"Laurel Landry." She stuck out a callused
hand. "I've got two tangos on my tail. They're
locked and loaded. I lost them a few miles back,
but they'll catch up. Sooner rather than later, I'm
guessing."

"Who's that?" he asked, gesturing toward the
dog.

"Sammy. My partner."

She had no more gotten the words out of her
mouth when a high-riding pickup pulled into
the parking lot. Two men climbed out. They
were loaded for bear with pistol-grip Mossberg
twelve-gauge shotguns at the ready. The twelve-

gauge shotguns would take down a grizzly. He didn't want to see what they could do to a man.

The bigger of the two men, who held his weapon with casual ease, pushed his way forward and addressed Mace. "No sense beatin' round the bush. Let us have the woman and we'll kill you fast, rather than take our time with it." Nicotine-stained teeth flashed in what Mace supposed was the man's version of a grin.

Mace knew the lady was waiting for his reaction. Did she expect he'd just hand her over? He widened his stance. "Not gonna happen."

"What's she to you?" the man challenged, shifting his grip on the twelve-gauge ever so slightly.

"None of your business. And I take it real personal when someone says they're gonna kill me. Fast or slow."

The one doing the talking was clearly the leader. The hard look in his eyes spoke of a lifetime of bad choices and bad company. He stank of sour sweat and cigar smoke.

Mace switched his attention to the second man.

He was twitchy and shorter by several inches than his partner, with the compact, dense muscles of a wrestler or football running back. That spelled strength, but it also might mean he didn't move as quickly as his leaner companion.

His head swiveled back and forth, and he

shuffled from one foot to the other. Clearly, he ranked far down in the Collective hierarchy. Probably brought along for backup only. Dark hair sprouted around the armholes and neck of the camouflage-colored T-shirt he wore.

The first man aimed his weapon at Mace, an obvious show of power. Mace studied the man's hands. He'd always found that hands telegraphed a man's intention more than did the eyes. The man's hands were sweaty. He wasn't as calm as he pretended. Mace saw through the cocky facade to the fissures beneath.

He could use that.

"Whoever's paying you to do this isn't paying you enough," Laurel said, speaking for the first time since the men arrived.

"Yeah? What's it to you?"

"Only that if you're going to kill me, I'd like to know my murderer was getting a big payoff."

He grinned, a stretch of thin lips that held no trace of humor. "We're not gonna kill you. Just take you to some folks that'll pay us ten grand."

"I figure I should be worth at least fifty grand."

Confusion crossed his partner's face. "Fifty grand?" Outrage rimmed his words.

"It's like I said in the first place, you're not being paid enough. I'd take it up with your boss."

Mace edged closer to his goal, knowing that

Laurel was trying to draw the men's attention to give him time to get in position.

The second man shot the leader an accusing glare. "You said ten grand was it."

"Too bad," Laurel said, a pronounced drawl creeping into her voice. "I'm sure you could get more. Maybe you ought to call this boss of yours and demand a better deal."

"And maybe you oughta shut up," the first man said as he cut a hard look at his partner. "She's playing you."

Mace angled closer to the leader.

"But fifty grand…" A whine crept into the second man's voice. "Homer, that's a sight of money."

"What'd I tell you about using names? Now shut your trap and let's get on with it. We ain't getting nothin' if we don't deliver the woman."

Mace watched as the first man shifted his grip on the shotgun once more. He was getting ready to make his move. Mace telegraphed his intention to Laurel with a small nod. Not by so much as a flicker of her eyes did she indicate that she was following his progress as he closed the distance between himself and the man.

"Now!" he shouted.

TWO

Laurel and Mace had top-notch training on their side, while their opponents were sloppy and undisciplined but brought over 450 pounds of animal fat and pure mean to the fight.

Mace set his sights on the man he'd pegged as the leader and kicked the shotgun from his grip. It was now hand-to-hand. Mace had excelled at hand-to-hand in close-quarters combat training, but his opponent was no slouch and had Mace beat in the weight department.

"You think you're gonna take me down?" the man taunted, all the while keeping his head out of reach of Mace's fists. Could he have a glass jaw? The man had a tell. Before he advanced, he wet his lips. It was a small gesture, but it was there.

Mace saw his opening and made his move, neatly evading a blow to the kidneys. He used his opponent's tell to his advantage, waiting for it, then moving in with a swift uppercut to the man's jaw.

His guess was verified when his opponent's eyes went glassy, his mouth slack. Mace followed up with a blow under the nose, causing the man to drop to his knees.

His opponent wasn't finished, though. He got to his feet, muttered something under his breath, and advanced on Mace with unmistakable intent in his eyes. Mace aimed a short-armed punch to the goon's face.

Striking the idiot in the face felt good, especially after he'd suggested that Mace abandon Laurel. He spared a glance in her direction and saw Sammy anxiously waiting for the command to attack. The command didn't come. She flashed Mace an I've-got-this look and fought with the ferocity and skill he'd expect of an Army Ranger.

His man got to his feet once more, swiped blood from his mouth and sent Mace a look promising retribution. He grabbed hold of Mace's arm and did his best to yank it out of the socket.

Mace wanted to give Laurel a thumbs-up, but he was too busy taking down the thug who was fixated on tearing him apart limb by limb.

"Nobody bests me and lives to tell about it. Not that we were gonna let you live in the first place."

"Enough." Growing tired of the man's taunts,

Mace did a roundhouse kick, aiming for his ample gut. When he went down, Mace knelt by him, saying, "Stay down, why don't you, and save yourself some pain."

The man spat at him. Mace grabbed a pair of flexi-cuffs from his back pocket and shackled the man's hands.

He turned to see Laurel still grappling with her opponent.

"Homer always thought he was so smart. But look who's still standing. I'll take you back in pieces if I have to," he said to Laurel, "but you'll be alive. You'll be real alive."

Mace started to step in, but Laurel stopped him with a feral grin. "He's mine."

He saw that her man had tossed aside the shotgun and pulled a knife, clearly not wanting to kill Laurel, just subdue her. They squared off from each other.

Mace hadn't pegged her as someone to back down from a fight. He was right.

The gleam of metal flashed menacingly through the air, but Laurel didn't retreat. Instead, she moved like a blur of motion, stepping into the sweep of the knife's arc and twisting the man's wrist, breaking his hold on the hilt of the knife. It fell from his grasp, and she kicked it out of the way.

"Want to try again?" she asked.

Enraged now, he bared his teeth and charged at her, head first. She spun, then gave him a kick to the pants that sent him toppling to the asphalt parking lot. She put a knee to his back and pulled his arms behind him.

Mace handed her a spare pair of cuffs. "You've got some moves on you."

After securing her man, she planted her hands on her hips. "What do we do with these yahoos?"

Mace pulled a length of rope from the bed of his pickup, tied the men back-to-back, and then bound their feet for good measure. "That should hold them until S&J gets the police on the horn and has them picked up." A quick text to Shelley took care of the matter.

"Get your gear," he said to Laurel. "I'll have one of S&J's operatives retrieve your car."

She grabbed her backpack from her vehicle and headed to Mace's truck.

He swung in the driver's seat while Laurel slid in the passenger side and Sammy bounded over the seat to the back.

"Ever been on Mr. Toad's Wild Ride?" he asked.

"Can't say that I have."

"Well, hold on. 'Cause we're gonna take it now."

With a squeal of tires, Mace peeled out of the parking lot. The narrow road wound its way through the valley then climbed steadily. Though navigating it required concentration, his mind wasn't on the road but on the woman sitting at his side.

The tight set of her shoulders told him she was tense but wasn't going to voice her worry aloud. Her sharp gaze was fixed on the road ahead.

"You've got some moves on you. You handled yourself like a pro back there," he said.

She sent an unsmiling look his way. "I *am* a pro. I did the same training as you, Ransom. No one cut me slack because I'm female."

"It shows." She was as well-trained as any soldier he'd fought alongside. "Sorry."

"Because you thought I was a poster child for women in the military and didn't have what it takes to back it up?"

"No. I never doubted you had the goods. What I didn't know was whether you traded on them, expecting special treatment because you're a woman. Now I know that you don't."

Her nod was curt. "Apology accepted."

"Where'd you pick up your friends?"

"Somewhere over the last ridge. I'd hoped I'd lost them, but they kept on coming." Her voice took on an edge.

He didn't bother telling her not to worry. She'd be a fool if she wasn't scared, and this woman was nobody's fool. A woman who'd made Ranger was exceptional. He'd known plenty of men, good men, who hadn't been able to make the grade.

The three-legged dog was another mystery. Obviously well trained, the dog was probably military. Military dogs were heroes in their own right. They had been instrumental in taking down bin Laden. If Mace were to guess, he'd say Sammy had been an explosives-sniffing dog, probably losing his leg doing just that.

"Sammy's ex-military, right?"

She nodded. "He lost his leg searching a building for explosives. He found something and refused to leave until he'd let his handler know. He saved my life that day plus six of my teammates." Her eyes darkened. "Three didn't make it."

Her terse explanation didn't pretty up the facts, though it had obviously cost her to recount that day. The affection between her and the big shepherd was palpable.

Mace darted a glance her way, then quickly looked away when he saw her bowed head. Though she didn't say anything, he knew she was praying. While he respected, even admired, believers, he couldn't agree with their faith. His own faith in the Lord had died during his years in Afghanistan. What kind of God allowed the atrocities he'd witnessed to take place?

Laurel looked up. "I apologize if my praying made you uncomfortable."

"No problem."

She slid her gaze over him. "But you're not a believer?"

"It's not that I don't believe. It's that I can't."

To his relief, she didn't pursue the subject. She folded her hands in her lap and went still. Despite her energy and skills, she had a restful quality to her that he appreciated.

Once again, he experienced a jolt of attraction. That kind of reaction wasn't typical for him, and he didn't like it. Didn't like it at all. Only one other time had he felt such a pull toward a woman and look at how that had turned out.

He resisted putting a hand to the scar that bisected his right cheek. No sense in drawing attention to it. Not that anyone could miss it. The scar, courtesy of a terrorist's knife, was the least of his wounds. The left leg that would never be fully functional again came from time in a POW camp.

But even that paled compared to the scars that marked his soul. From long habit, he pushed away the spiraling downward turn of his thoughts and focused on the client at his side.

Beauty was in the eye of the beholder, but this lady would make any man sit up and take notice. Flawless skin was complemented by heavily fringed eyes and a mouth that looked like it might have curved in a smile easily enough had the circumstances been different. As it was, her lips were firmed in an uncompromising line.

He didn't fault her for that. Having two of the Collective's foot soldiers on your tail tended to take the fun right out of you.

She held herself tightly, the tense posture saying more than words could that she was preparing for a fight. Her eyes blazed with the rush of adrenaline, and he knew his did as well.

"Relax," he said. "I haven't lost a client yet."

His lame attempt at humor didn't raise so much as a small smile from her.

"Sorry." She lifted a shoulder in a shrug. "It's been a pretty intense twenty-four hours."

"I get it."

After that brief exchange, she lapsed into silence.

Laurel understood that she was being vetted by the bodyguard. She didn't mind. Much. She was doing some vetting of her own and decided that Mace Ransom was a straight shooter who didn't waste time. She appreciated that. A complicated man, she judged.

He was tall, with a rangy build that spelled both strength and speed. Along with jeans and Frye combat boots, he wore an Under Armour shirt and a tactical Blackhawk Warrior Wear jacket system. She guessed there was a holstered weapon beneath the jacket.

His no-nonsense clothes echoed her own. With the temperature steadily dropping in the deep woods, she was grateful for her Duluth Trading jacket, flannel shirt, jeans and Asolo hiking boots.

She turned her attention away from his clothes to the man himself. A bladed nose, sharp cheekbones and narrow-set eyes hinted of Native American ancestry. It wouldn't be surprising. Many people in the South bore a trace or more of Cherokee blood. All in all, it made for a compelling face.

His features were too rough-hewed, his eyes too full of determination for the bland good looks that found favor in the glossies and online e-zines. No, Mace Ransom would never be mistaken for a movie star or a media idol.

He was closemouthed but could ask questions when he wanted to know something. Even if she hadn't known he was an ex-Ranger, she'd have made him as spec-ops. It was there in the smoke-colored eyes that missed nothing, in the ramrod posture with the resolutely set shoulders.

His bearing shouted military. She liked the reassurance of that, the familiarity of it. Everything about him was hard. Hard eyes. Hard hands. Hard driven. She'd been around such men for the last nine years of her life. They didn't give in and they didn't give up. For that, she was grateful.

The scar on his cheek didn't repel her. She'd

seen worse. Far worse. Along with a day's growth of beard that roughened his jawline, it added to the dark and dangerous appeal of the man. She bore her own share of scars, some visible, others not. Stars and scars, one of the men in her unit had used to describe spec-ops soldiers.

There was a faint indentation on his chin that might have been a dimple if his lips were to curve in a smile, but the harsh lines bracketing his mouth told their own story, that of a man who rarely if ever smiled. Had life in the Rangers turned him bitter and angry or was there another explanation for the dark cast to his face?

He bore not a lick of the gloss that had characterized her onetime fiancé, though he had been military, too. Jeffrey had been all spit and polish on the outside. It was a pity that he'd been so ordinary on the inside. Laurel pushed memories from her mind of the man who hadn't been able to handle her making Ranger when he'd washed out.

Unless she missed her guess, there was evidence of a deeper kind of pain in Mace Ransom, the kind that shadowed the heart and the soul. She saw it in the darkening of his eyes when he turned her way and the tight control with which he held himself. At the same time, she detected a steady kind of valor in his eyes, the kind that said he'd do what was right, regardless of the cost to himself.

Whatever put the pain in his eyes, it was not her problem. Or her business.

She wasn't there to psychoanalyze the S&J agent. She needed his help. Ever since the explosion that had injured her shoulder, she had been functioning at half speed. She needed to step up her game.

"If I didn't say it already, thanks. For coming. For being here."

"No need. I go where the job takes me."

Okay. That put her in her place. She was an assignment. "Still, I appreciate it. I've handled myself in plenty of tough situations, but this has me rattled."

As if sensing her distress, Sammy nudged her neck with his nose. She reached back to scratch his muzzle. "It's okay," she murmured. His wet tongue laved her cheek, the small gesture of affection warming her.

"He's a good animal," the man at her side observed.

She let her nod answer for her, afraid that her voice would break if she said that Sammy was far more than that.

She returned to her study of the bodyguard. He deserved to know what he was up against. "The tangos on my tail belong to the Collective."

"I've been briefed." His face hardened, along with his voice.

"Just wanted to make sure we're on the same page."

"Gotcha. The Collective doesn't play nice with others."

"No kidding? I think they murdered my mother." She left it at that. There'd be time enough later to go into details, that Bernice's throat had been slashed, nearly to the bone.

Sammy nudged her with his nose.

"Do you need to go out?" The shepherd gave a sharp bark, and she turned to Mace. "Can we stop?"

He pulled to the side of the road. "Make it quick. Unless I'm wrong, there'll be others on your tail besides those two idiots back there."

She hopped out of the truck, let Sammy out. He spent a minute sniffing the grass before settling down to business.

"Good boy." She patted her leg. "I wish we could let him run," she said as Mace joined them. "He's not used to being cooped up."

"Sorry. We've got to keep moving."

His words triggered a nasty memory. While she'd been deployed in Afghanistan, her unit had been assigned to take down a munitions dump. They'd succeeded but had taken fire, leaving a couple of men wounded, which had slowed them down. A small band of the enemy had managed to escape into the hills and then proceeded to track Laurel and her men relentlessly, intent on revenge. They had lost a man in the ensuing fight.

"Believe me, I know."

Mace didn't fool himself into thinking that they were home free. There were bound to be others tailing his newest client.

He wasn't often taken by surprise, but Laurel Landry had managed to do just that. Instead of the hard-edged female Ranger he'd expected, he saw a beautiful woman with auburn hair, golden eyes and a soft mouth.

Not that she was soft. She handled herself like the professional soldier she was.

It was that dichotomy that intrigued him.

The big shepherd stayed at her side. Having only three legs didn't lessen the fierce protectiveness he displayed when Mace made to help Laurel back in the truck. A sharp woof told Mace to back off.

"Sorry," Laurel said. "Sammy's appointed himself my guardian." She knelt and wrapped her arms around the dog's big neck. "It's okay. He's a friend." She gestured for Mace to put out his hand to Sammy, who sniffed it. "Friend."

"At the risk of offending Sammy, can I give you a hand?" Mace had noticed she favored her right shoulder.

"Sure."

"What happened to your shoulder?" he asked as she winced when reaching for her seat belt.

"I took shrapnel from an IED." When she didn't say anything more, he took the hint to back off from further questions.

On their way again, they talked little except to exchange ideas for the best route to Atlanta. He gave the lady credit for keeping conversation to a minimum. Small talk was not part of his skill set. It was the same for most of the soldiers in spec-ops. *You want polite chitchat, you join a ladies' garden society. You want results, you get yourself a Ranger.*

He eyed the Sig Sauer P226 that showed beneath her jacket. "Nice toy you got there."

"Thanks." She glanced at the Glock 17 he carried in a shoulder holster. "Same goes."

"It does the job."

Right now the job meant getting the client out of harm's way. He had no doubt that other men would pick up their tail quickly enough. With that in mind, he sifted through the choices. Keep to the back roads, hoping to fly under the radar. Or hit the freeway with the idea of losing themselves in the mix of vehicles heading east. Each came with a risk.

Part of his Ranger training was evaluating risks. A county road or the freeway? A county road was less likely to be patrolled by the tangos. On the other hand, there was safety in being able to lose themselves in the hundreds of vehicles that filled the freeway like an army of ants.

The freeway it was.

He took the ramp and merged into the steady stream of impatient drivers. Middle-of-the day traffic was only slightly less congested than that of early morning or late afternoon. He switched lanes, moving into the right where slower vehicles were directed. He had no problem going fast—none at all—but the slower pace would make it easier to spot a tail.

"You're pretty cool for having been chased by thugs," he said.

"Getting upset isn't going to change things. Besides, it uses energy I may need on down the road."

She was right about that. They weren't out of the woods yet, and despite her calm words, he knew she was wound tightly. He saw it in the compressed lips and tightly clenched hands. She was likely running on fumes. When they gave out…

He shook his head at the probable outcome. Even a Ranger could go only so far without refueling. Adrenaline layered upon danger would have her crashing in an hour or so. He needed to get her somewhere safe, somewhere she could rest.

He glanced at her, noted the grayness of her

skin that spoke of exhaustion. Even with that and the shadows beneath her eyes, energy vibrated from her. "You don't say much."

"I figured you as the type who didn't appreciate idle talk."

"You figured right."

She lifted a brow. "Then what's the problem?"

"No problem. Just wondering what you did to make those yahoos so mad."

"Let's just say they woke up on the wrong side of the bed."

While he appreciated a woman who didn't chatter all the time, he was looking for answers. "What do you know about the Collective?"

"Not as much as I'd like. I know Ronnie Winston's been in federal lockup for the last year."

"You came prepared," he noted.

"When someone's killed my mother and chasing me, I tend to take it personally."

"How'd your mother get involved with the Collective?"

Laurel didn't answer and, instead, asked a question of her own. "Jake Rabb and Shelley Judd, they're brother and sister, right?"

He gave her credit for having done her homework on S&J. "Right. Shelley and Jake are good people. If anybody can help you, they can."

"And you?"

"And me." When she yawned widely, he said, "Why don't you close your eyes for a while?"

"Why don't I?" She made a half turn to the back seat. "Sammy, time for rest."

Mace watched the exchange in the rearview mirror. Sammy relaxed his vigilant posture and stretched out on the seat, taking up the full length of it. A soft expression stole over Laurel's face as she gazed at the dog.

"He's special to you."

"Sammy's been through a lot and seen me through more. He's the best. There were some who said he ought to be put down after he lost his leg."

"Guess that didn't sit well with you."

Her partially closed eyes snapped open. Mace studied her. Weariness shrouded her, the lines fanning from the corners of her eyes deep, her smile there by an effort of will and little else.

"You guessed right. Sammy deserved better than that. He saved a lot of lives. In my book, that makes him a hero."

"In mine, too," Mace said, but her eyelids had drifted shut once more. He glanced over his shoulder at Sammy. "Don't worry, boy. We'll keep her safe."

If Mace hadn't known better, he'd have said that Sammy nodded his assent.

Mace maneuvered through traffic and considered S&J's newest client. Beautiful. Intelligent. Courageous. A woman who was being hunted.

Laurel Landry was an intriguing woman, but

she was a client and, as such, hands-off, even if he was attracted to her.

While in Jalal-Abad, he'd met an American woman working as a schoolteacher. Teachers were often in danger in Afghanistan and he'd admired her dedication to her students. Attraction had bloomed between them and, for the first time in his life, he'd found himself falling in love. It was a heady sensation, and he savored it.

He'd thought she returned his feelings, that is until he learned that teaching was a cover for her CIA job. Though the Army and the CIA occasionally worked together, their goals were often opposed. Any feelings for her had died when he discovered that she was using their relationship to advance her own agenda.

He'd learned his lesson and learned it well. He had no time for women now. Everything he had, everything he was, he gave to the job.

The job came first. Always.

THREE

Laurel awoke with a start, her thinking fuzzy as she tried to recall where she was. A glance at her watch had her groaning. She'd slept two hours.

Sammy! A shot of fear cleared her mind, and she started to turn around in the seat when Mace's voice stopped her.

"He's fine. He's been snoring." A pause. "Same as you."

Her denial was instinctive. "I don't snore."

Mace flashed a grin. "Have it your way."

"I never sleep in the middle of the day." She needed to make that clear.

"You've probably never had members of the Collective on your tail either."

"There is that." She stretched. "I didn't realize how tired I was until…"

"Until now. I get it. Adrenaline got you so far, then you crashed. It happens."

"Thanks."

"For what?"

"For not making a big deal of it."

Another flash of that grin. "You're the one doing that."

He was right. There was no need to apologize for her body's need for rest. "Still, thanks."

He waved that off. "We need to stop and gas up."

Her stomach rumbled. "I could go for some food."

"You got it." He jerked the steering wheel to the right and exited the freeway.

It was then she noticed the men following them. "Got company," she said.

Mace didn't take his eyes from the road. "Let's see how good you really are with that Sig."

She drew herself up as far as possible in the limited confines of the truck. "I can shoot the wings from a gnat and send them flying."

"Well, then, is your arm broken?"

Laurel grabbed her Sig, the feel of it as familiar as her own hand.

She turned in her seat, rolled down the window. There was still the possibility that the driver wasn't part of the Collective, just an innocent man who happened to be going the same direction they were, so she held her fire.

A bullet found its way into the upholstery, putting to rest any doubts. Firing from a moving vehicle took precision and timing. Television shows and movies made it look ridiculously easy.

The truth was that only one in twenty marksmen could take out a tire in such circumstances.

Though she was a crack shot, she didn't go for a tire but the engine. A bigger target increased the success rate exponentially, and a bullet hitting the engine could start a nice little fire, enough to keep the tangos busy for a time. She lined up her target and fired.

The ping of metal against metal told her she'd hit her mark. Seconds later, flames burst from the engine. "Nailed it."

"Not bad."

Laurel noted that Mace didn't drive directly to a restaurant but took several detours as the two of them looked for any additional tails. Forty-five minutes later, he pulled into the parking lot of a diner that had seen better days but was still trying. The pockmarked parking lot, where enthusiastic weeds grew between the cracks and a tired-looking sign promised home cooking, spoke of hard times.

Mace circled the lot. Laurel approved the precaution and paid attention to the location of windows and exits.

Sammy whined.

"Just a minute, boy, and I'll take you on a walk and get you some food and water."

Mace parked the truck by the rear door. "Might as well not advertise that we're here."

She nodded in approval. It wouldn't take much

deductive reasoning to figure that she and Mace would be looking for food and fuel. Mace at her side, Laurel took Sammy for a short walk, then set out a bowl and put food in it. She opened a bottle of water and filled his water bowl.

When Sammy finished, the three of them walked into the diner. She paused to talk to the man behind the counter. "Okay if I bring my dog with me?"

The man darted an impatient expression her way until he saw Sammy wearing his service dog vest, and whatever he'd been about to say died on his lips. "No problem. I recognize a soldier when I see one."

"Thanks. I appreciate it."

He tapped his chest. "Marines. First Gulf War."

"Rangers," she said, pointing to Sammy and herself.

As though she and Mace had rehearsed it, each performed a grid search, doing a threat assessment. Laurel took the right half, noting a pair of teenage girls who couldn't take their eyes off the boys in the next booth, an older couple who reached across the table to hold hands, a young woman nursing a cup of coffee. No one appeared menacing, and Laurel relaxed fractionally.

She watched as Mace performed his own search. Apparently he, too, didn't notice anything out of the ordinary for he took her elbow and steered her to a booth at the back.

They vied for the coveted position of back-to-the-wall. The wry grin he gave her told her he knew what she was thinking and was amused by it. In the end, they sat side by side so that they both had their backs to the wall. Sammy took position at Laurel's feet.

The smell of deep fat frying filled the air.

Mace opened a grease-stained menu. She did the same and eyed the limited choices. They both ordered meatloaf sandwiches and mashed potatoes with gravy. The food was plentiful and surprisingly good. Laurel ate every bite and considered ordering a slab of pie as well. She hadn't eaten since last night and discovered she was ravenous.

"You're sure you've had enough?" The quirk of his lips caused her own to twitch.

"I'm thinking of getting a piece of apple pie."

"Go for it."

She did, washing down the warm pastry and fruit with a chocolate shake. Fifteen minutes later, she sat back, lips curved in satisfaction.

"A full belly makes the world look brighter," he observed, an appreciative smile breaking over his features.

"Spoken like a true soldier." Her smile died as she considered the fact that she might no longer be a Ranger, not if the rehab for her shoulder failed.

"Now suppose you tell me what you did to get someone so riled up at you."

She leaned forward, braced her elbows on the table and propped her chin on her hands. "I was home on medical leave when I got word that Bernice—my mother—had been killed."

Mace listened, saying little, only nodding occasionally. All the while, he was processing what she told him, fitting it in with what he already knew about the Collective.

"Why your mother?"

"Bernice is...was...an attractive woman. In addition, she knew her way around a spreadsheet. She didn't have much in the way of formal schooling, but she could work wonders with numbers. It's likely she caught some man's attention, and he discovered she could keep books and keep her mouth shut at the same time." Her lips twisted at the last.

Mace noted that she referred to her mother by her first name. He filed that away, to be taken out and examined later.

"When she stole the ledger and the money, she sealed her fate." The lack of emotion in Laurel's voice as she spoke of her mother's murder intrigued him almost as much as did the fact that the woman had worked for the Collective.

"How did you find the ledger and money? It makes sense that whoever killed her went through her things to find them."

"I think they did. The trailer was a mess when I arrived. Bernice wasn't the world's best housekeeper, but she'd have never left flour on the counter the way I found it. She couldn't abide weevils and that's a sure way to attract them. I think the people who killed her looked for the ledger and money, then ran out of time when I showed up at the trailer for the funeral."

"Still doesn't tell me how you found them."

"There was a receipt and a key for a storage locker in the pocket of a dress. I almost missed it. I went to the storage place and found her go-bag in the locker."

At his raised brow, Laurel explained, "Bernice always kept anything of value in an old suitcase, her go-bag. No matter how many times we moved when I was growing up—and there were a lot—she took that suitcase with her. It was ugly as all get-out. I remember asking one time why she kept it and she told me that it wasn't any of my business.

"I had to wonder what made that suitcase so important that she had to rent a storage locker for it when she barely had two nickels to put together." Laurel rubbed her arms, as though suddenly cold. "That was when I discovered the ledger and money."

"You made sure you weren't followed?"

She gave him a what-do-you-think look. "By that time, I was feeling pretty paranoid. So, yeah, I made sure I wasn't followed to the locker. Or I thought I did." Her face scrunched into a frown. "But I guess I wasn't as careful as I thought because a man was waiting for me when I started to leave. I took care of him, but Homer and his buddy picked up my tail. You know the rest."

Considering she had narrowly escaped two sets of gunmen intent on killing her, the lady looked remarkably calm. "Tell me about making the Rangers."

If she was confused by the change of subjects, she didn't let on. "I earned my place like any other soldier. But nobody could leave it at that. They had to make a big to-do over it."

"You have to admit that a female Ranger is news."

"I wanted to be a Ranger. Just that. Not a *female* Ranger. Just a Ranger."

He could all but see the impatience chafing at her. "Why does everyone have to goggle? I'm a woman. I'm also an Army Ranger. In my mind, the two fit just fine. The fuss the bigwigs in the Pentagon, not to mention the idiots in the media, make of it makes me see red."

Mace respected that, even admired it, but she was being naive if she thought women in the

Rangers weren't going to attract attention. "Get over it. You're news."

"Yesterday's news." Her shrug belied the annoyance in her eyes. "Can we talk about how we're going to get out of here without taking company with us?"

"Company?"

She lifted her chin at the two men who'd just walked into the diner. There wasn't anything about them to attract attention unless you looked closely and saw the way they carried themselves, their arms held slightly away from their bodies to accommodate the weapons that were no doubt holstered at their shoulders.

He should have spotted it. Would have, but he'd been engrossed in Laurel and the puzzle she presented.

"Get up and act like you're going to the ladies' room. Then wait outside the door."

She didn't bother asking questions, only did as he said, Sammy trotting at her heels. When she'd exited the room, Mace signaled for the check. He paid it, added a generous tip, and then casually inquired about the shortest route to Washington, DC. The young waitress gave directions to the freeway. He nodded and thanked her.

He made his way to where the restrooms were located and found Laurel. Pushing open the door to the men's room, he made certain it was empty, then gestured for her to follow him inside.

"What do we do now?" she asked.

"We wait."

It didn't take long.

The larger man came in first. Mace grabbed him by the arm, twisted him around so that he fell heavily against the sink. The thug reared back, but Mace was ready and slammed the man's head into the stained porcelain. The man gave a single grunt, then made a "no more" gesture. Mace whipped out flexi-cuffs from his back pocket and quickly bound the assailant's hands together.

Sammy growled, and Laurel smoothed her hand over his hackles. "Next one's mine."

"Go for it."

When his buddy didn't return from the restroom, the second man showed up. "Virgil?" He gave the door a cautious push. "Virge, you there?"

Laurel waited behind the door.

Mace nudged his captive with a none-too-gentle kick to the ribs. With the barrel of his gun pressed against the man's head, Mace whispered, "Answer him. No funny business."

After a grimace, Virgil called out. "Yeah. I'm here."

"Hey, Virge, what's taking so long? I expected you to come back with a couple of war trophies—"

Laurel didn't give him time to finish. She

yanked the door back, sending the second man off balance. When he stumbled, she kicked out with her right leg, catching him in the gut.

He grunted in pain but didn't topple.

She followed up with a blow to his jaw, then slammed the ridge of her knuckles under his nose. It bled profusely.

"You're gonna—"

"Pay for that? That's what they all say." She hooked her leg under his, and, with a twist of her hips, threw him to the ground. Positioning her foot against his neck, she said, "Tell us who sent you."

The man twisted his neck to shoot her a look of hatred.

Virgil got his bravado back. "You ain't gettin' nothin' from us." Despite the defiant words, the man looked like he didn't think for himself and waited on others to tell him what to do. A nose that had been broken at least twice did nothing to offset a mouth that had several teeth missing.

"No?"

"Maybe this will help. Sammy, show 'em your stuff." The skiff of fur at Sammy's neck stood at attention, and he gave a grumbling growl.

"I ain't scared of no three-legged dog," the second man said even as he shrank away from Sammy.

"Sammy is a decorated soldier. He knows

twenty ways to kill you. All it takes is a command from me and you'll be dead within seconds."

A man walked inside, took a look at the scene before him and quickly backed out.

"Tell us who sent you or I'll leave the lady and her dog to finish you two off." Mace made a sound of disgust. "And maybe I'll put it out there that the two of you were taken down by a woman half your size and her three-legged dog."

Neither man said a word. Laurel knelt beside them and searched their pockets. "Nothing. Not even a cell phone."

Though the men didn't appear overly smart, they'd had brains enough to leave their phones behind. A phone's history could yield a wealth of information.

Mace pulled out his own phone and sent a text to Shelley, explaining the situation. She would smooth things over with the local cops who were sure to show up in quick order. A grin pulled his lips up at the corners when he got a reply.

What's up with you? Can't you go a couple of hours without getting into it with the Collective's thugs? Shelley had never held back on voicing her opinion.

After slipping a pair of flexi-cuffs on the second man, he hauled both men into the far stall and dumped them on the floor. "These two won't be going home tonight."

Sammy gave a last growl at the men.

"Keep your freak of a dog away from me," Virgil muttered.

"What? Now you're afraid of my three-legged friend?" Laurel gave a short command to Sammy, who sat back on his haunches, then aimed a look of contempt at the men. "You're the worst kind of cowards. Sammy served his country bravely. You two wouldn't know the first thing about that."

Mace wadded up paper towels and stuffed them into the men's mouths.

"C'mon," he said to Laurel. "If the police get here before we leave, we're in for a bunch of questions. I want to put a whole lot of gone between us and whoever is after you."

"You read my mind."

Mace hustled them out the back door. Rain spat from angry clouds, thin drops sharp with teeth that slashed at the skin.

Laurel climbed into the truck, Sammy on her heels. Once inside the cab, she heaved out a breath.

Mace drove out of the parking lot at a leisurely pace just as two police cars were pulling in.

Her sigh of relief echoed his own feelings. Though he believed in cooperating with the locals whenever possible, he hadn't wanted to stick around. If it was the Collective who was after her, they were bound to have more men in the vicinity.

"I'd have liked to question those two some

more," she said, frustration ripe in her voice, "but they're like the others, obviously low-level, probably don't even know who sent them after us."

She was right. The men hadn't appeared to have the intelligence or the initiative to act on their own.

She angled herself toward Mace. "What now?"

"We keep heading for Atlanta." He slanted a curious look in her direction and asked the question that had nagged at him since Shelley had told him of the assignment. "Why S&J? There had to be other security firms you could have hired."

"I did some research and liked what I learned about S&J, especially that it's made up of ex-military and law enforcement. In my book, that says a lot."

The answer made sense. Yet he had the feeling there was more to it than that. He stored that away.

"I'm sorry about your mother."

"Don't be. We weren't close."

It was a cold answer, but he sensed there was more to it than what the few words conveyed. The expression in Laurel's eyes told him that she wasn't going to say anything more, at least not then. Another mystery.

None of his business. All he cared about was keeping her safe and learning whatever she knew about the Collective.

"You must be really important to have the Collective send three teams after you in one day."

"You'd think so, wouldn't you?" Her lips lifted in a wry smile. "I'm beginning to think that the Stand was safer than Georgia."

He grinned at her use of the military's slang for Afghanistan. "You might be right."

Mace's smile died as memories assailed him. He'd returned to the States a different man from the callow boy he'd been when he'd enlisted.

He had watched buddies die, put up with orders that made no sense from politicians who had never stepped foot on a battlefield, and been betrayed by the woman he thought he loved. He'd endured all that and more.

But it was the unspeakable cruelties he'd witnessed that had soured his stomach and destroyed his faith.

FOUR

Mace sifted through impressions of his client. Strong. Stubborn. Full of secrets. Everyone was entitled to secrets. Including him. Especially him. He wouldn't hold having secrets against Laurel, unless those secrets put him and her in danger.

The truck's interior was too small to contain the tension that shimmered through the air. Granted, he and Laurel had just fought off yet another attack, but it was more than that. There was a coiled anticipation in her that made him want to stop the truck here and now and demand that she tell him what was going on. He pulled at his collar to rid himself of the cramped sensation, but to no avail.

Laurel must have found a safe place for her thoughts to inhabit as she didn't attempt to break the silence that pulsed between them. Which was fine with him. He wasn't ready to give voice to the maelstrom of thoughts that swarmed through his mind. He was still coming down from an adrenaline high, as he suspected she was doing, too. Taking on two tangos spiked the senses, then came the crash.

With an effort, he focused on the present. He had a job to do. Deliver Laurel to Atlanta and keep her safe.

After several attacks on her life in the last few hours, it was quickly becoming clear that keeping her safe meant stopping the Collective. From what he knew of the organization, it would hunt her relentlessly and then exact a price of retribution.

He could ask Shelley to assign another operative as Laurel's bodyguard while he worked the investigative end of things. If that meant taking down more goons like the last ones, well, that was all right by him. His lips tightened at the idea of men hunting her as though she were an animal.

Laurel would demand that she work with him. Though they'd known each other for only a few short hours, he already understood that she wasn't one to stand on the sidelines. What had he expected? She was a Ranger, after all.

A frown worked its way across his face. The Collective wouldn't go down easy. The members would fight with their last breaths, and they'd fight dirty. Did she know what they were capable of?

As soon as he posed the question, he had his answer. Of course she knew. She'd fought in Afghanistan, saw firsthand the inhumanity that hatred spawned. In the Stand, fear and cruelty ruled.

There were instances of exceptional courage, both on the part of American personnel and that of the Afghani people, who were, by and large, honorable and devoted to their families. It was the warlords and insurgents who had corrupted the country with ever-growing intimidation and terror. Their thirst to inflict their extremist beliefs upon others was unquenchable.

He'd put the horrors of that war away, only to sign on with S&J and take on a different kind of war—protecting innocents from those who would prey on them.

He had to convince Laurel to let him do the investigating while she remained in a safe house. Knowing that she'd undoubtedly raise a ruckus over that didn't solve his problem. He worked best alone. Always had. He'd tell her, let her down easy. Maybe now would be the right time.

Before he could explain to her why she couldn't work with him, she said, "You're trying to figure out how to tell me that you're going to cut me loose when we get to Atlanta and investigate on your own. Right?"

Caught, he nodded. "Something like that."

"No way, Ransom. I'm in. All the way. It's my life on the line."

"S&J doesn't let clients work with operatives."

Even as Mace said the words, he knew he wasn't being completely truthful. Other S&J operatives had worked with their clients, and four of those operatives were now married to those same clients.

Not that he had anything to worry about on that score.

"It's a safety thing," he said, wincing at the lame-sounding words. "Shelley Judd will assign another operative to act as your bodyguard, and I'll start investigating. We'll keep you safe and put an end to the Collective at the same time."

"You really think S&J can stop the Collective?"

"I don't know," he said honestly. "But we can put a big dent in the organization." Of that, he had no doubt.

He'd seen S&J's operatives bring down some pretty big fish, including corrupt federal prosecutors, greedy union bosses, and dishonest newspaper publishers. When it came down to it, they were all the same: predators who stepped on others to get what they wanted.

"Why should you do the investigating?" Laurel asked, returning to the subject he preferred to leave behind. "Why not leave it to someone else?"

He had his answer ready. "I was with military

police before I made Rangers." That was weak, but he couldn't tell her the real reason: he was attracted to her, so much so that he feared he'd lose his objectivity. The sooner he handed her over to another operative, the better.

For both of them.

"And I've had CID training," she said. She didn't add "so there," but she might as well have.

The Criminal Investigation Department of the Army was among the best-trained law enforcement in the armed services. "When?"

"Before I made Ranger. I wanted to get as much experience under my belt as I could."

"You must have started young."

"I enlisted when I was eighteen." A small shrug. "Seemed the right thing to do."

She'd managed to surprise him. Again.

"We'll be in Atlanta in another hour. You can tell your story to Shelley and Jake and we'll take it from there."

"Thanks for all you've done."

Mace shrugged that off. "Save it for when I've actually done something."

"You saved me from those lowlifes the Collective sent after me."

"You and Sammy did a pretty good job of saving yourselves."

Her gaze touched his, but for only a moment, before it darted away and a blush stole up her cheeks.

He'd spoken the truth. He had no doubt that

Laurel could have taken on the teams of men by herself with Sammy as backup and come out on top. She had grit to spare. He liked that about her. In fact, he liked a lot of things about the lady.

The direction of his thoughts startled him. As though to negate them, he shook his head, refusing to go down that rabbit hole. As they said, *Been there, done that.*

Laurel wanted to do a happy dance in her excitement about meeting Jake and Shelley. At the same time, she wanted to weep for the years she had lost with them. Her brother and sister. She felt it. There would have to be tests, but her gut told her she was right.

She and Mace had made the rest of the trip to Atlanta with scarcely a word spoken between them. She was too wrapped up in anticipation, and Mace had lapsed into a brooding silence, the edge of a frown putting the beginning of furrows on his brow.

At her request, he had taken her to a hotel and, after checking in, she'd cleaned up, fed Sammy and then taken him for a walk.

Now, as she sat in Shelley's office at S&J headquarters, she absorbed impressions of Shelley and Jake. They had an easy kind of give-and-take relationship that made her think of the families she'd dreamed of when she'd been a little girl.

Jake was tall and rangy while Shelley was petite, a bundle of energy that made her seem larger than her five-foot-nothing frame. Jake took his time making up his mind and spoke with slow deliberation; Shelley made snap decisions and didn't mind letting everyone know what she thought.

Like two adjacent pieces of a puzzle, they fit. Would there be a place for her? Laurel wondered. Or was the puzzle an exclusive one, made only for two? She steered her thoughts from that emotional quicksand and concentrated on the present.

After introductions were made, including giving Sammy time to sniff Jake and Shelley and decide that they were all right, Laurel explained what had brought her here.

Concluding her story, she gestured to her backpack. "I have the ledger and money here. I didn't want to leave it at the hotel."

"Smart move," Jake said.

Shelley leaned forward. "Can we take a look?"

In response, Laurel opened the pack, withdrew the ledger and money and handed them to Shelley.

Shelley flipped through the pages of the ledger. "Obviously encoded. We'll put our encryption specialist on it." She passed it to Jake.

While he looked at it, Shelley thumbed through a packet of hundred-dollar bills, a corner of her lip caught between her teeth. "Not a fortune," she said, "but enough to steal." At that, she flushed. "I'm sorry. I didn't mean that your mother—"

"It's okay," Laurel said and, like Shelley, tucked the corner of her lip between her teeth. "I'm pretty sure she stole the money. That's probably what got her killed."

"I'm sorry," Shelley repeated, and Laurel heard the sincerity behind the two words, "for your loss."

Laurel shook her head. "We weren't close." Familiar pain pushed its way forward. As always, she pushed back.

Thoughts of Bernice and how she'd died intruded. Bernice, who'd always chased happiness with the wrong men. She'd played the victim card and attracted men who wanted to make her just that. In the end, it had gotten her killed.

Laurel caught the shared looks between Shelley and Jake and found herself not wanting to lie to them, to pretend that the relationship between Bernice and her was that of a loving mother and child.

Questions she'd parried throughout childhood and her early teen years came back to taunt her. Questions like "Why doesn't your mom come to your school play?" and, worse, "Why is your mom so mean to you?"

She told herself that none of that mattered now and changed the subject. "I want in on the investigation. I was with CID for a time before I joined the Rangers. I can help."

Mace bunched up his mouth, as though trying to contain the words that were itching to get out. When he finally spoke, it was in a carefully neutral tone. "I already told her that we don't involve clients in the investigation. It's too dangerous."

Shelley steepled her fingers together. "With her background, Laurel could be an asset." She turned an expectant gaze on Mace.

Mace trained cool eyes on Laurel. "Boss lady says you're in, you're in." A muscle at the base of his neck flexed even as a flicker of annoyance skimmed over his face.

Laurel heard the reluctance in his voice and knew that while he wasn't happy about the decision, he'd abide by it. Though he'd left the Rangers, he was still a soldier and that was what soldiers did: follow orders.

"Thank you," she said to Shelley. "Thank all of you. I'd be grateful if you could keep the money and ledger here. I don't want to carry it around with me. Too risky."

"Good idea," Shelley said. "I'll put them in our safe."

Mace stood. "Laurel's dead on her feet. I'm taking her back to the hotel where she can get some shut-eye."

Shelley gave Laurel a sympathetic look. "Of course. Don't worry. Mace will keep you safe."

Outside, Laurel realized how late in the day it was. The sun slid like melted butter below the horizon. On the drive back to the hotel, she closed her eyes, taking in all that had happened. Shelley and Jake were everything she had hoped for. And more. You had only to gaze into Shelley's eyes to see the integrity shining there. The same went for Jake.

But something had held her back from telling them about the photo and sharing her belief that she might be their half-sister. She chewed on her lip when she recognized the source of her omission. Fear. She'd never lacked courage when it came to taking the fight to the enemy, but she was afraid to confide in Shelley and Jake.

Laurel had endured Bernice's rejection, but she wasn't at all certain she could bear rejection from the man and the woman who might be her brother and sister.

Had anyone noticed that Shelley had a habit of tucking a corner of her lip between her teeth, the same as Laurel?

She opened her eyes to find Mace watching her.

"What did you think of Jake and Shelley?" he asked.

She blinked. What did he mean? Had he guessed... No. She was jumping to conclusions. "I liked them."

"They're pretty great," he agreed. "They had

a rough childhood, but they've made something of themselves, something good."

What would it have been like to have grown up with such a brother and sister? She tamped down the longing in her heart and reminded herself that she was here to find answers, not to moon over what might have been. And she had Sammy, the best partner she could ask for.

As though aware of her thoughts, Sammy nuzzled her neck.

"You look far away," Mace observed.

"No further than my thoughts," she said lightly, though those thoughts were anything but light.

"Care to share?"

"No." Afraid she'd sounded abrupt, she tacked on, "But thanks." For right now, she'd hold her thoughts to herself.

"No problem."

Only it was a problem. She, who had always prided herself on her honesty, was lying to the man who had saved her life and to the brother and sister she longed to call her own. She understood why she hadn't yet told Jake and Shelley the truth, but why not Mace?

The answer came swiftly. She didn't want to put him in the position of having to keep something from his bosses who were also his friends.

Mace ran a dispassionate gaze over Tony the Snitch. Tony was a slight figure who was frequently overlooked, which made him all the better at slipping in and out of places and ferreting out information.

Tony had earned his nickname legitimately. He sold what he learned on the streets...if you could meet his price. He had his fingers in a number of pies, including running errands for people who knew people. He moved in and out of the shadows with the certainty that no one would stop him. He provided a valuable service and took pride in it.

Mace had used the CI for several years now. Confidential informants—good ones—were worth their weight in gold. Tony was a sneak and a thief and would as soon sell you out as he would breathe, but he delivered the goods.

After settling Laurel in the hotel and ordering room service for the two of them, Mace had arranged for another of S&J's operatives to stand guard outside her room. Guilt nagged his conscience as he thought of the intentional omission.

He told himself that Laurel needed rest, but that wasn't the whole truth. He preferred working alone.

He had slipped out of his room and driven to the seamy side of the city, where back-alley deals were made with the same finesse as those in the upscale financial district. That the traders wore chains and leather rather than Brooks Brothers made no difference.

He preferred the first to the second, hands down. At least the chains and leather traders made no pretense of being anything other than what they were, unlike the Brooks Brothers–clad businessmen who hid behind facades of civility and polish.

Now he stood in one of those back alleys, with the intention of trading money for information. Steam rose from the concrete, turning the air thick and murky. A sliver of moon cast eerie shadows. The stench of overripe garbage permeated the night.

Mace ignored the stinging in his nostrils as he did the gang graffiti that covered every surface. Guilt scratched at his conscience as he thought of leaving Laurel behind. He soothed it with the reminder that she needed rest.

In his experience, security/protection jobs had prolonged periods where things moved at a glacial pace intermixed with intense action. With Laurel, there'd been few times of inaction, only continuous engagement with the enemy. He wanted to take advantage of the lull and get a handle on what he was dealing with.

Tony slunk out of the shadows. Quick as a snake and twice as crafty, he was whip thin with an oily edge that made Mace want to wash his hands after dealing with the man. Now, Tony hedged and dodged Mace's questions about the Collective.

"You know me," Tony whined to Mace in a

singsong voice that was his trademark, "I don't mess with the Collective. They're bad news."

Tony had his share of faults, but he had always been on the up-and-up with Mace. So when Tony said he didn't mess with the Collective, Mace believed him.

As Tony fidgeted, Mace dug in his wallet for a fifty-dollar bill. It was a game where both parties knew the rules. Tony pretended not to know anything; Mace coaxed out what he needed by flashing cash under Tony's nose. In the end, both got what they wanted.

"The Collective's been active lately," Mace said, easing Tony into the conversation by slipping the fifty into the man's grimy hands.

"Word on the street is that someone took somethin' they want back. They want it back real bad like."

"Any idea of what that something is?"

"Some money. Maybe ten grand. But that ain't the big thing. It's a book." Looking genuinely perplexed, Tony scratched his head. "I don't know why they're all worked up over a book. Can't be worth much, least not to my way of thinkin'."

The ledger. That had to be it. Mace kept his excitement to himself. "What makes this book so important?"

Tony lifted a scrawny shoulder. "Don't know.

There's a reward for it." His eyes lit with greed. "A big one. No questions asked."

"If somebody came across this book, who should they contact about it?"

"That's where it gets tricky," Tony said. "No one wants to deal with the Collective. Like I said, it's bad news."

"What about the money? Any reward on it?"

"Yeah, but the book is worth a whole lot more."

"You hear anything else, you let me know. Right?" Mace held out another fifty, which Tony deftly snatched and pocketed.

"Right."

Satisfied that he'd learned all that he could, Mace headed back to his truck just as a figure stepped out of the shadows.

Laurel.

FIVE

Features drawn into a scowl, Mace fisted his hands on his hips. "What are you doing here?"

Deliberately, Laurel imitated the gesture, picturing two gunslingers preparing to draw down on each other in a B Western. "Don't patronize me, Ransom. I'm Ranger-trained. Just like you. I can handle myself."

"So I saw. But that doesn't change the fact that you're the client and I'm the operative."

A punch of sound punctured the night. With an effort, she kept from flinching. A car's backfire. Not a gunshot. Not an explosion in an abandoned school in Afghanistan.

Her heart settled, and her breathing returned to normal. Almost. The humidity pressed against her, slicking her skin with the sticky warmth of a Georgia summer.

She raised a brow. "What do you think? I heard you leave, so Sammy and I slipped out the door of your room since you thoughtfully provided a guard for mine. I waited until he was checking his phone, caught a taxi, and told the driver to follow your truck." A smile found its way to her lips. "I've always wanted to say that."

"You shouldn't have come. This isn't exactly the best neighborhood."

Her brow lifted another notch as she recalled her posting in Jalal-Abad where nightly shootings, knife fights and even explosions were the norm. She rolled her lips between her teeth in a bid for patience. "Sammy and I have seen worse." Automatically, she smoothed her hand over Sammy's neck. "What did your snitch tell you?"

"How do you know I was talking to a snitch?"

"I worked CID," she reminded him. "I know a snitch when I see one. Had a couple of my own."

"He didn't have much, but he did tell me that there's a reward for the return of the money and the ledger."

She licked her lips. "The Collective must be desperate to get their hands on that ledger."

"That's what I thought. The sooner we get it decoded, the better."

"We're working together. No more going off on your own." She tapped a finger against his chest. "Got it?"

Mace caught her hand, stilled it. "What I do on my own time is my business."

A zing of awareness started at her fingertips and raced up her arm at his touch. Without giving the gesture more importance than it deserved, she removed her hand from his grip. "You and I are joined at the hip until we figure this thing out."

"You're a hard lady."

"No harder than I have to be."

He nudged her to the truck.

She climbed in, Sammy following. "Tell me what else you learned."

Mace started the ignition. "That's it. Tony'll get back to me when he knows something more. In the meantime, I want you off the streets. Don't forget—the Collective has put a bounty on you."

She angled herself so that her gaze met Mace's. "I won't let it keep me from doing my job."

"You hired S&J. That makes it my job."

She made a circling motion with her finger. "And here we go again, back to where we started. I'm sticking with you like white on rice. Get used to it."

Laurel didn't hear Mace's response as the rapid report of M4s reverberated through the night. The hiss of a bullet between her and Mace was too close for comfort. It buried itself in the dashboard. A couple of inches either way would have been a different story.

"Stay down." Mace was already reaching for his Glock.

Laurel didn't bother responding. She drew her weapon, opened the door and crouched behind it. "Stay," she commanded Sammy after making certain he had jumped to the floor of the truck.

Sammy gave a sharp woof but obeyed like the soldier he was.

Two men were advancing on them, firing repeatedly. Bullets stitched across the driver's door, then the front and back tires, and finally worked their way to the truck's engine block. Mace dove beneath the truck and rolled to the other side. Laurel steadied her aim, fired and hit one man in the shoulder. She wanted him alive.

Mace trained his gun on the second man.

The man must have decided not to risk taking on two opponents by himself, for he pivoted, causing Mace's shot to miss by a hair, then retreated, ignoring his partner's cries for help.

Just when Laurel thought he was going to make a clean getaway, he raised his weapon, but he didn't aim in Laurel or Mace's direction. He fired at his partner, hitting him squarely in the chest, then in the head.

Kill shot.

The shooter jumped into his vehicle and took off.

Mace ran to the downed man, Laurel at his heels. He bent and felt for a pulse, then shook his head.

"I wanted him alive," Laurel said, disgust thick in her voice.

"The very reason his partner shot him," Mace added.

His grim tone echoed her feelings. If they'd taken the man alive, they could have pumped him for information, which was exactly why his partner had killed him.

Laurel had seen her share of death—more than her share—and still felt her heart clench at the coldly executed murder. There'd been no hesitation on the part of the shooter. He'd taken out his partner with no more thought than he would have given in squashing a bug. Bile scorched the back of her throat. With an effort, she swallowed it back.

The breath she expelled reminded her that she was still alive. The prayer she silently uttered reminded her that it could have been her or Mace lying in the filthy street.

At Sammy's whine, she let him out of the truck. He circled the body, then came to stand guard at her side. Like her, he had seen too much death.

Mace punched in 911. There'd be no avoiding questioning by the police. Not this time.

When a patrol unit showed up, he gave a thumbnail sketch of what had gone down. He and Laurel caught a ride to the precinct station in one of the squad cars and answered questions from a detective without giving away anything. *Tell the truth but don't volunteer information.*

No, they didn't know the men who had attacked them.

No, they didn't have any valuables on them that would warrant a robbery.

Yes, they'd stay available for further questioning.

At 2:00 a.m., it was business as usual. In working for S&J, Mace had spent more time than he would have liked at police stations. Each bore the same smell of old coffee and industrial cleanser, with an underlayment of despair.

He pushed back his chair and stood. "If we're done for now, I want to take the lady back to the hotel," he said and then realized that his truck had been towed away.

"I'll have one of the unies take you." The police detective followed Mace's frowning gaze to where Laurel sat.

Mace resisted the impulse to brush his knuckles over her cheek, to comfort both himself and her. The paleness of her face concerned him. If she didn't get some rest soon, she'd collapse.

Sammy had stayed by her side during the hour-long session of questions. A low growl warned others to keep their distance.

"That's a fine dog you have there," the detective said. "Looks like he's ex-military."

"He is," Laurel said. "He earned a Purple Heart."

"My brother lost an arm in Iraq. He has a service dog now, also ex-military. That dog is the best thing that could have happened to him."

Laurel shared an understanding smile with the detective. "I hear you."

Mace cupped a hand under her elbow. "Let's go."

Outside, he breathed deeply. Even the humid Georgia night air was better than the recycled air of the station house. Sweat gathered at the nape of his neck and trickled down his back. During the firefight, he'd been calm, even cool. Now all he felt was a hot anger that he and Laurel were once again targets.

"I'm getting tired of wearing a bull's eye on my back," Laurel said, echoing his feelings. "How did they find us this time?"

"I'm guessing the same way that Tony knew about the reward for the ledger. Money talks. Pass enough of it around and somebody's bound to collect on it. You and that book appear to be worth a bundle."

She fluttered her eyelashes at him. "You sure know how to sweet-talk a girl, don't you?"

Mace couldn't help it. He laughed. "You beat everything, you know that? You've been hunted by the Collective, shot at multiple times, questioned by the police. And you still manage to make me laugh. What's it take to get you down?"

Her expression sobered. "You'd be surprised."

Not for the first time, Mace wondered what had put the worry in her eyes. Certainly she had reason for it. She'd gone through a bunch of bad stuff—starting with learning of her mother's murder and then locking horns with the Collective on multiple occasions—but he sensed there was something more. Something important. Something she refused to tell him.

It made him all the more determined to discover her secrets. If somebody gave him a puzzle, he just had to solve it.

Laurel Landry was definitely a puzzle.

Laurel concentrated on putting one foot in front of the other.

Except for the couple of hours of rest she'd grabbed on the way to Atlanta, she had been going flat out for more than forty-eight hours. If she didn't get a few hours' sleep, she'd be no good to anyone. Including herself.

Mace ought to have been equally weary, but his face held only cold determination as he checked out her hotel room. "Can't be too careful."

For the last two days she'd been putting one foot in front of the other in an attempt to do what needed to be done. Now, she didn't know what she would be called on to face tomorrow. Or the day after that.

The what-came-next pushed at the edges of her mind because she didn't know what it was. The not knowing was harder to bear than the pulse-pounding action of facing down bad guys and trying to stay alive.

Mace stopped, frowned, eyebrows pulled tightly together. "You look lost."

His words yanked her back to the present. "I feel lost." She swallowed at the admission. She was a Ranger, had undergone some of the most intense training there was in the armed services, but she didn't know where she was going next.

"It'll be okay," he said. "You aren't alone."

She grasped on to the words.

"Get some rest," he said and then walked through the connecting door to his room.

Tired as she was, Laurel knelt at the side of the bed, bowed her head and said a prayer.

Talking to the Lord was something she did throughout the day. When she'd joined the Army, she realized how much she relied on Him and His constant care. He'd seen her through too many life-threatening situations to count and had never let her down.

She knew many in the Army and the Rangers who were not believers. It saddened her, but at the same time, it made her more grateful than ever for the faith that sustained her. She hadn't learned about the Savior's love at home. A friend had invited Laurel to attend church with her.

Her first experience at a service had filled her with such peace that she'd known she had to return. The warmth of joining others in worship, through prayer and song, kept her returning until she'd become a regular at church, volunteering when she was old enough to help teach Sunday school class for the younger children.

The prayer soothed away the rough edges of the day.

Feeling more in control, she shed her clothes, stepped into the shower and attempted to wash away the violence and ugliness of the last hours. When she finally lay down in the king-sized bed, she expected to fall asleep within minutes, but sleep did not come easily, and when it did, it was punctuated with nightmares. She thrust them away until one grabbed hold and refused to give up its grip on her.

She awoke screaming.

Something wet laved her face. She sat up with a start, hand groping for her weapon, before realizing that it was Sammy.

"Sorry, boy," she said. "I was screaming, wasn't I?"

Gun in hand, Mace burst into the room, his eyes darting about. "What is it?" His jeans and shirt were obviously pulled on quickly, his hair sleep mussed.

"Nothing." At his look of disbelief, she added, "Except a nightmare." No sense in pretending otherwise. "The IED." Five seconds that had changed her life forever.

For the first few weeks following the explosion, she'd woken in the same way, always with a scream. The nightmares had stopped, for the most part, but the events of the last two days had triggered another one.

Shards of memory wrapped their way around her, jagged edges pricking her from all sides. She breathed deeply, a vain attempt to dislodge the hold they had on her.

Sammy whimpered softly, a sound that managed to be both inquiring and comforting at the same time.

Looking around the hotel room, she anchored herself there, in Atlanta.

The Army shrink she'd been ordered to see had said that stress was her enemy. She gave a short laugh. All she had to do to de-stress her life was take down the Collective, find a way to tell Shelley and Jake that they had a sister and get her shoulder to heal.

No problem.

No problem at all.

Mace tucked his weapon into the waistband of his jeans. "You gonna be okay?"

"Yeah." That was a lie. But a girl had her pride. And right now that was the only thing keeping her going.

"You want to talk about it?"

Did she? Did talking about the nightmares imbue them with more power? She didn't know.

She checked the time on her cell—nearly 5:30 a.m. She wouldn't be going back to sleep. Maybe she did need to talk to someone, someone other than an overworked shrink who had too many patients and not enough time.

"How about breakfast in thirty?" she asked.

Mace nodded. "Sounds good. Meet you in the dining room."

Exactly twenty-five minutes later, freshly showered to wash away the sweat of the nightmare, she sat across the table from Mace in the small dining room of the hotel. She'd noticed Mace had conducted a grid search of it. She'd done the same and deemed it safe.

"On time was considered late in my unit," she said by way of explanation.

He nodded. "Same here. My sergeant used to say that if you only wanted to be on time, join the navy."

Laurel laughed, feeling the release of tension. "I hear you."

He placed his big square hand over hers and squeezed it.

The contact was minimal, but she felt the warmth seep into her, a quiet knowledge that she wasn't alone. So startled was she by the unexpected gesture that she looked at their linked hands to confirm it. She kept looking at them for longer than was warranted, noting the contrast in size, the texture and color of skin, the pressure of his fingers against hers.

All made her intensely aware of his strength. Of him.

She couldn't help comparing him to Jeffrey, the man she'd believed she might someday marry. Jeffrey had always needed to make himself seem bigger, better, smarter than he actually was, a futile attempt to make up for what was lacking inside.

Mace had no need to puff himself up. He was comfortable in his own skin and didn't need to rely on outward trappings as Jeffrey had.

After their break-up, she'd wondered what she'd seen in him and concluded that she was so eager to find love that she'd been blinded by the image he presented. She was grateful she'd seen through his false persona before she'd taken the next step with him.

Sammy, who had waited patiently at her side for his food, gave a gentle woof. "Sorry, boy," she said. She dug his bowl from her backpack, filled it with a bag of food she also kept there and said, "Mind your manners. We're in a hotel."

Sammy looked at her in reproach, as though he already understood that he was in a hotel and would use his best manners, so why was she reminding him of it in the first place?

"He's a winner," Mace said.

"He is that. I'm fortunate that I could adopt him. Sammy wants to be needed and he knew that I needed him."

"You two make a good team."

"The best." She went quiet, thinking of how Sammy had come into her life at just the right time.

As though sensing her reflective mood, Mace said, "Your unit saw some action in the Stand."

"Yeah. We did."

Her commanding officer had said that the Stand separated soldiers from wannabes. He hadn't dismissed her with a wink and a smirk as did some of the officers. *There is no gender in Rangers,* he'd said. *There are only those willing to serve and even to lay down their own lives in defense of their country.*

The missions had been rough, and her last one had cost three men in her unit their lives, Sammy his leg, and Laurel the use of her shoulder. When this thing with the Collective was over and if she was still standing, she intended on visiting the families of those men. Those mothers and fathers, wives and children deserved to hear firsthand how their sons, husbands, and fathers had died fighting for something they believed in.

She'd held her own and had come away with a medal and the respect of the men she'd served with. Medals weren't important. The respect of her fellow soldiers was. It was that to which she'd clung during the long weeks in the hospital and the longer weeks in rehab.

Memories assailed her with the same piercing heat now.

Weeks of rehab followed the surgery to remove the shrapnel. She'd approached rehab as she would a mission: tough her way through no matter the cost.

She didn't realize how long the silence had stretched until Mace said, "About last night—"

"When you ditched me and went out on your own?"

"I should have told you what I was doing. You're right. From now on, we work together."

Surprise rippled through her. "Thank you. I'm sorry about your truck."

He made a gesture of dismissal. "The truck's toast. S&J has leased one until I get around to buying a new one." A pause. "Want to tell me about the nightmare? I'm a good listener," he prompted.

Image after image flashed through her mind with relentless clarity. Darkness followed by blinding light. Deafening noise. A high-pitched wail that seemed to last forever.

Why wouldn't it stop?

Shrapnel of nails, screws and razors exploded all around her. Torn flesh. The acrid odor of explosive materials. Blood had dripped from her uniform—hers and that of a buddy. Automatically, she pressed her hands to the gaping wound in his gut.

Dark blood continued to spurt. She recognized *death blood*. Still, she kept up the pressure, willing the young soldier who'd pushed her out of the way to live. It wasn't enough. He'd died in her arms.

Before she realized it, she was talking, a spit of rapid-fire words. "I'd seen men die before," she concluded, "but this was different. He gripped my arm so hard I thought he might break it. I kept telling him that help was coming, that he'd be all right." She stopped, momentarily ambushed by memories of the unspeakable waste that was war.

"He wasn't. I must have passed out. I don't remember being carried out of the school. I woke up four days later in a hospital at Ramstein," she said, naming the air base in Germany.

Mace didn't offer sympathy, only a nod of acceptance.

"Thanks for listening. Maybe I can put it away."

They both knew it was a lie.

SIX

Mace understood Laurel's reluctance to talk about the explosion that had wounded her and taken a comrade's life. He rarely shared his own experiences of the war. Too much pain. Too much ugliness. Too much disillusionment.

When he'd returned to the States, he'd resolved to put away that part of his life. His lips twisted. He hadn't been any more successful than Laurel had sounded.

The desperate look in her eyes told him she wanted to drop the subject. He was happy to comply. Anything to wipe away the shadows under her eyes. Though she'd slept, she didn't look rested.

"I have something to show you." Laurel pulled her laptop from her backpack, inserted the thumb drive and handed the computer to Mace.

He skimmed the file, his face darkening. It outlined the Collective's activities in the Southeast over the last five years. The organization had its hands in every type of crime, from money laundering to human trafficking to selling illegal weapons and dealing in drugs.

"Where did you get this?"

"I have a contact in the DOJ. I reached out to him on my way to meet you. He sent me some intel. The FBI has the goods on the Collective. Why isn't it doing something?"

The frustration in her voice echoed his own, but Mace knew how things worked, knew that the Collective had tentacles that found their way into every sphere, including law enforcement itself. No one was beyond its reach.

There was an additional reason the Bureau had been slow to act. "With a dozen new hot spots popping up all over the world every day, unless you can connect something to a terror nexus, it gets shifted to the bottom of the pile."

"That's just it." She clenched her hands, unclenched them. "This *is* connected. Along with selling illegal weapons in America, the Collective is branching out to selling stolen weapons to arms dealers who aren't picky about whom they sell to."

"Like terrorist cells."

Her nod was short, her voice clipped. "Just like."

Abruptly, he switched subjects. "Tell me about you and your mother. I notice you refer to her as Bernice. Any special reason why?"

Laurel folded her napkin and set it on the plate. "I hadn't seen her in over a decade."

"Why?"

Now Laurel pushed back from the table. "She didn't want me. She told me that from the minute I was old enough to understand. I was a nuisance. I always wondered why she kept me around. Later, I realized she could just use me for welfare money."

Mace didn't rush to offer sympathy or to dismiss her feelings. Instead, he said only, "That must have been rough."

"You could say that." Pain shadowed her eyes. "Why do you do what you do, first the Rangers and now working for S&J?"

It was a question few people had asked, one he rarely asked himself.

He could give the easy answer: that he was protecting a way of life, the one that politicians idealized and poets immortalized. But it went deeper than that.

When he'd started high school, a boy several years older than him had been in his grade. It hadn't been hard to understand why the older boy, who must have been sixteen or more, was in the same grade with a bunch of fourteen-year-olds. He became the butt of bad jokes and cruel comments.

Mace did his best to stand up for Roy, even taking on bigger boys who persisted in taunting the boy. With that, Mace became Roy's protector. Mace had brought trouble on himself, but he'd refused to back down. His father had supported him, giving Mace one of his infrequent words of praise when he'd received a black eye defending Roy from two bullies.

When Mace's father had been killed in a factory accident, Mace had taken on the role of head of the family, though he'd been only sixteen. He'd managed to hold down two jobs while still maintaining a 4.0 GPA. At eighteen, he'd enlisted in the Army, eventually joining the Rangers.

"You were going to tell me why," Laurel said.

"I don't like bullies. Doesn't matter where they are or who they are, I can't abide them. What's going on in the world comes down to some people bullying others."

She nodded. "I get it."

"I wanted to make a difference in the world. Fighting America's enemies seemed like the way to do it. I spent some time in a POW camp, came away with a bum leg. It's mostly okay now, but I knew I couldn't go back to the Rangers." He thought of her injured shoulder and tipped his chin at it. "Do you ever regret it?"

"Not for a minute. How about you? Do you regret it?"

"Not for a minute."

In accord, they finished their breakfast.

Mace pushed back from the table and stood.

"I want to check in with Shelley and Jake, fill them in on what happened last night."

Laurel stood as well. "Sounds good."

Outside, they found a truck waiting, courtesy of Shelley's efficiency. He'd called her last night and explained about his truck. He hadn't gone into details, only to say that the vehicle was inoperable. Shelley had messengered keys to him.

He took the loss philosophically. It wasn't the first truck he'd sacrificed while on the job; it probably wouldn't be the last.

Fifteen minutes later, Mace was sitting in Shelley's office. Laurel had taken Sammy outside, so Mace and Shelley were alone. The once efficiently streamlined office now resembled a nursery with riding toys, stuffed animals and a high chair fitted among the filing cabinets and desk.

Mace smiled at the picture of Chloe that sat prominently on Shelley's desk. "Chloe looks more like you with every day."

"And I think she looks like Caleb. He spoils her ridiculously. The other day he took her and one of her little friends to the park. I warned him what he was in for. When they came home, he looked shell-shocked and said he'd been on missions that were less hairy."

Mace's smile stretched wider at the thought of former Delta Caleb Judd now a doting father taking his tiny daughter and friend to the park. "I'd have liked to have seen that."

At one time, Mace had wanted his own share of the American Dream, a wife, family and home. When he'd considered the realities of that dream, though, he wondered about the consequences. He thrived on the thrill of a mission successfully executed. Would knowing that a family was waiting for him cause him to temper the risk taking that made him such a good operator?

The answer was simple: of course. Could that get him or one of his buddies killed? Maybe.

It was an idea he had relegated to cold storage, rarely taking it out to examine. In Jalal-Abad, a woman had tempted him to believe he could make his dream a reality...before he'd discovered her duplicity. Fortunately for him, no woman since had found her way into his life.

He filled in Shelley on last night's adventure. "If only we could have taken him alive," he said, referring to the man who had been shot.

"I know how you feel. But even if you'd taken him alive, it might not have done any good. The Collective has its foot soldiers acting independently of each other. They're operating like terror cells. No one group knows more than it has to. Makes it real hard to trace things up the food chain."

Mace acknowledged that with a dip of his

head. Shelley was right. Maybe he wouldn't have learned anything from the man, but he'd have liked to have given it a shot.

"What do you think of our newest client?" she asked, switching subjects abruptly. Though S&J believed in hiring topflight people and then staying out of their way so they could do their jobs, Shelley ran a tight ship and knew the names and details of every client, every job.

"She's the real deal, handles herself like a pro and keeps her head when the bad guys are closing in."

"But…" Shelley prompted.

"She doesn't give much away," he said evasively.

"Come on. I know you have an opinion."

"She has a lot of broken spots inside of her. The problem is, that's where she thinks they should stay."

Shelley's lips quirked. "Pot and kettle, Mace?"

He felt a slight smile pull at his own lips. "Maybe. A little. And maybe that's why I can recognize it in somebody else."

"You've got a point." Shelley's expression sobered. "I like Laurel. But you're right. She has broken pieces, like most of us. And she's holding something back. Something important."

Holding things back could cause problems if it had to do with the job. Holding things back could get you killed.

* * *

Laurel looked from Mace to Shelley and back. They'd been talking about her. She was certain of it. Maybe it was time to come clean. When Jake walked in, she made up her mind. Quietly, she told them of finding the picture and the news clippings about S&J along with the ledger and the money.

Laurel passed the items to Shelley. "I'm not asking you to believe me on face value. Just that you listen and then check it out."

Gazing at the first picture, Shelley clapped a hand to her mouth, then turned to Jake. "It's us. You and me. I remember that dress I was wearing. It had little ducks embroidered on it." Her voice grew husky. "How old would we have been here? I look about seven. That would have made you fourteen, right?" Shelley gazed at the second picture, where Bernice stood alone. "That's her. Our mother." Her lips twisted on the last two words.

"Even after all these years, I recognize her." Shelley tapped the photos. "She left not long after these were taken." She turned to Jake. "Do you remember? She told us she was going to the store and never came back."

Jake's nod was grim. "I remember. She'd borrowed money from a loan shark and couldn't pay it back. He came looking for her."

Laurel watched the exchange with growing empathy for Shelley and Jake.

"Jake fought tooth and nail when they wanted to split us up in foster care," Shelley said.

"What happened?" Laurel asked.

"We were placed together. When Jake was old enough, he got us out of there and took care of both of us until I was old enough to be on my own."

Shelley handed the pictures to Jake, who ignored them. Instead, he knelt in front of his sister and took her hands in his. "So she has a couple of pictures. She could have gotten them anywhere. We don't know—"

"It could be." Laurel heard the tentative hope in Shelley's voice. "It could be."

"Asking us to believe that we shared a mother is a lot," Jake said, turning to Laurel, eyes hard as his voice.

"What about the pictures and clippings?" Shelley asked.

"They don't prove anything" He started to crush them.

"No!" Shelley grabbed them back. "They don't belong to us. They belong to Laurel."

"Why did you come here? Dredge all this up?" Jake demanded of Laurel. "We didn't need the woman who called herself our mother then. We don't need any reminders of her now." Unspoken was the claim that they didn't need Laurel either.

Laurel didn't shrink from the words. She held her ground, as she'd been taught in the Army. "I don't blame you for not believing me. I should have said something sooner. It's just…"

"Just what?" Shelley prompted softly.

"I wanted to get to know my brother and sister." A hitch in her voice betrayed just how much she wanted that.

Up until then, Jake had appeared unmoved by her story. With his arms folded across his chest, he looked every inch the ex-Delta she knew him to be. Now his expression softened. "I get that you want a family. I won't fault you for that."

Though Shelley barely topped five feet, she was a dynamo of action. Now she paced back and forth. "It took courage for Laurel to come here. I say we give her the benefit of a doubt."

Laurel flashed Shelley a grateful smile. "Thank you. The last thing I wanted was to hurt you." She divided a look between Jake and Shelley. "Either of you. But I wanted to meet you." She shook her head at her phrasing. "I *had* to meet you."

"Why?" The single word, baldly said, came from Jake.

"I went through my life thinking there was only her, a woman who made it plain she didn't want me. I wanted…" She cleared her throat, shook her head once more. "It doesn't matter."

"I think it does. You were looking for family." Shelley reached for Jake's hand.

The small gesture arrowed straight to Laurel's heart. An uncharacteristic wistfulness overtook her before she shook it off.

She looked helplessly at the brother and sister she hoped to call her own. Jake was right— she didn't have any real proof, only a gut-deep feeling that she was right about her relationship with him and Shelley. So maybe that feeling was borne only out of longing; that didn't mean she was wrong.

She needed proof. They all did.

It was clear Jake was withholding judgment, equally clear that Shelley wanted to believe her. Laurel drew in a breath as resolve stiffened her shoulders. "However you feel about me, it doesn't change the fact that the Collective is still active, still murdering people."

"And you're on its hit list." Shelley came to a halt. "Laurel gave us valuable intel." She sent Jake a reproving look. "Whatever brought her here, I'm grateful. We might have a sister."

Laurel said a silent prayer about what she should do next. The Lord had never let her down. Sometimes, though, He allowed her to work things out on her own. She figured this was one of those times.

Revealing who she was to Shelley and Jake

had been harder—infinitely harder—than she'd thought possible.

Well, what had she expected? A woman they'd met only a day before announces to them that she could be their half-sister. Anyone would have been skeptical, especially Jake and Shelley, who had no reason to believe that the mother who had abandoned them had another child.

"We need to do DNA tests. But..." Laurel smiled tremulously. "The pieces fit." She turned to Mace, who had a way of studying her as though waiting for an opportunity to peel back another layer. "What do you think?"

"This is what you've been hiding." It wasn't a question.

"Yes."

"Okay."

"Just okay?"

"Yeah."

Laurel realized she had blindsided not only Shelley and Jake, but Mace as well. It couldn't be helped, but she heard the censure in his voice that she hadn't been honest with any of them.

She opened her backpack and booted up the computer, pulling up the file she'd shown Mace less than an hour earlier. After giving everyone a chance to skim it, she said, "You see it, don't you? The Collective's growing increasingly violent and is now selling weapons to our enemies."

Jake's expression grew grimmer by the moment, as did Mace's.

"One of the locals who volunteered in our unit when I was stationed in Afghanistan described what war had done to his country as scorched earth, leaving nothing in its wake," Mace said. "That's what the Collective does. It's a cancer. After the attacks on Laurel, it's clear that they won't stop until she's dead. If we want to keep her alive, we have to put an end to it. She'll never be safe otherwise."

"So what's the answer?" Laurel asked.

Silence.

Laurel chewed on her lip. When she looked up to find Shelley doing the same thing, she couldn't help but laugh, despite the serious nature of the conversation.

Shelley joined in the laughter, and even Jake smiled. "The DNA tests will prove what I already feel," she said to Jake as she grabbed hold of Laurel's hand. "We have a sister."

"We *might* have a sister," Jake cautioned, but his voice no longer contained its earlier harshness and he eyed Laurel with a considering look.

Laurel gave thanks that he wasn't rejecting her outright.

While the others talked, Mace considered what Laurel had told them. Her secretiveness and evasion made sense now. From remarks Shelley and Jake had made, he knew that their mother had neglected and then abandoned them. Apparently the woman had not changed her ways when it came to mothering. No wonder Laurel had described their relationship as "not close."

He recognized the root of his suspicions. The woman he'd fallen for in Jalal-Abad had deceived him in the worst way possible. Though he'd long since gotten over any feelings he'd once had for her, the sense of betrayal had eroded much of his trust in others, especially women.

"What's our next step?" Laurel asked, dividing a look between him, Jake and Shelley.

"We learn everything we can about the ledger," Jake said.

In response to that, Shelley pressed a button and called in Rachel Martin, S&J's encryption expert. Within a few minutes, the woman appeared. Mace had met her a few times and been impressed with her skills. A former FBI agent, she now led S&J's cyber section.

After making introductions, Shelley outlined the facts of the case and, after removing the ledger from the safe, showed it to the specialist. "We need this translated ASAP."

Rachel looked through the pages. "Looks like some kind of binary code."

"That's what I thought," Laurel said, "but I couldn't make any sense of it beyond that."

"I'll do my best," Rachel said to Shelley.

Shelley smiled warmly. "I know you will."

After Rachel left, Shelley said, "If anyone can do this, Rachel can. She's a whiz kid, graduated from high school at fourteen, finished a four-year degree in eighteen months, did grad work at Harvard, and was then scooped up by the Bureau."

Mace had heard rumors that Martin had left the FBI under some kind of cloud. Not his business. He turned his thoughts back to bringing down the criminal enterprise.

"So, how do we put an end to it?" Laurel asked.

Mace didn't have to think about it. "We cut off the head."

"Ronnie Winston?" Jake asked. "He's already in prison."

"But he's still giving orders." Mace gripped the edge of the desk. "That piece of trash is finding a way to lead the Collective. Behind bars, and he's still calling the shots. If we cut off his line of communication to the outside world, it would put a big dent in the Collective's operations."

"We don't know who he's communicating with." Frustration ripened in Shelley's voice. "After you called," she said to Laurel, "I checked the prison logs. No one but his wife has been to visit him. No one's written him."

"I want to meet him," Laurel said.

"Not a good idea," Mace said. "Winston's bad news."

"Hey," she said and tapped her chest. "Ranger here. Remember?"

"Yeah. But..." He looked to Shelley and Jake for help.

"Maybe Laurel will learn something nobody else has," Shelley said.

Jake only lifted a shoulder.

"I can hold my own," Laurel said. "Just before my last mission in the Stand, my team and I hunted down a warlord. I'm not going to let some Collective boss intimidate me."

Mace didn't bother arguing his point again. "We'll arrange it. Just remember—you asked for it."

SEVEN

Before meeting Winston, Laurel wanted to do some homework on him. Aside from what her contact at the DOJ had sent her, she knew little about the man and wanted to understand his endgame. Knowing what the opponent desired above all else was key to predicting the next move.

The tactic had worked well when she'd led a unit in Afghanistan to take down a band of insurgents. She and her fellow soldiers had determined that the terrorists needed ammunition and would likely try to overtake a munitions bunker thirty-five klicks to the west. Her unit had been waiting.

"Okay if I use my computer here?" she asked Shelley.

"Sure. I'll set you up in one of our loaner offices."

"Loaner office? Like a loaner car?"

Dimples winking, Shelley grinned. "Just like."

She showed Laurel to an office and gave her the Wi-Fi password. "Work here all you want."

"Thank you." Laurel settled in at the desk and pulled up all the information she could find about Winston and the Collective.

Over and over, she read "Not enough evidence to take to authorities" in reference to further crimes committed by the Collective after Winston's arrest and conviction.

That segued to the problem Mace had named. Even with sufficient evidence, who could S&J and others working on taking down the organization give that evidence to? With judges and prosecutors in the Collective's pockets, the possibility of the evidence being thrown out of court was too big to calculate.

Laurel made notes of her own, wrote down impressions and questions that needed follow-up. Her thoughts circled back to Bernice's involvement with the Collective. What had she done to warrant her murder? Stealing the ledger and money, certainly. But had there been something more?

Laurel stopped, considered. Maybe it wasn't what Bernice had done but what she'd learned. Bernice hadn't been above using information or people for her own benefit. Had she tried to blackmail the wrong person?

Ronnie Winston had spent the last twelve months in a federal lockup, but he was still the puppeteer, possessing enough power to order others to do his bidding.

From what Laurel had learned about the Collective, nothing happened without his okay. So how had Winston given the order to kill Bernice and then tried to do the same to Laurel? She returned to Shelley's office, where she found Mace and Jake, and posed the question.

"How does a prisoner who receives no visitors, no mail, no contact with the outside world manage to control something as far-flung as the Collective? What about Winston's wife?"

"Everybody from the DA's office to the police looked, and looked hard, at his wife, but there was nothing there," Mace said. "She appeared to be completely in the dark about his activities."

"I've got a friend in the DA's office," Jake said. "He told me that there wasn't a shred of evidence to connect her to anything."

"So how's he doing it?" Laurel persisted.

Brother and sister looked to each other and grimaced in unison. Mace's gaze was fixed on the floor.

"There's more communication going on inside a prison than you'd believe," Jake said at last. "There's the old library book trick. Leave a message in a book, it's picked up by another inmate, one who does have outside contacts. But that's old-school. Prisoners today are sophisticated."

"How so?" Laurel asked. "Technologically?"

"Maybe. But that's risky in itself," Shelley said. "Technology leaves a footprint. No matter how well you cover your tracks, someone is going to find it. I've ferreted out more information from what people think they've deleted than you'd believe."

Laurel bit her lip as she pondered it. "So how do these sophisticated prisoners pass messages?" She was silent for a moment, trying to figure out how Winston was managing to get messages to his minions. "What does he do in prison? Work in the laundry room? Or the machine shop?"

"That's something we need to check out," Shelley said, "though I think Winston would keep communications away from where he's assigned to work."

"Then how is he doing it?" Laurel persisted.

"It can be as innocent as a meal tray," Mace answered. "Leave a little pile of vegetables at the top of your plate and you've just ordered a hit."

"How do they know who the hit is on?"

"That's where the code comes in to play," Jake said.

"Code?"

Mace nodded. "Sophisticated doesn't have to be high-tech. It just needs a code, one that the parties involved have agreed upon in advance. Winston's considered a big deal in prison. He probably sets the code, then tells others they'd better abide by it or else."

Laurel paced. "You're saying Winston can order a hit on someone on the outside just by playing with his food?"

"Something like that," Shelley said, tapping her fingers on her desk. "Three months ago, almost a year after Winston went to prison, a judge was murdered in his bed. He was one of the good guys and was presiding over a case against a Collective foot soldier. He'd received several warnings and had agreed to have the United States Marshals take his family into protective custody. They were moved to a safe house."

"And the judge?" Laurel asked.

"He refused to leave, said he'd be safe enough with two sets of marshals on the outside and inside." A beat of silence. "Turns out he was wrong. All four marshals were found with their throats slit. The hit man saved something special for the judge. He was garroted, after his tongue had been cut out.

"No one's dared speak against the Collective since."

Laurel recalled a particularly nasty band of insurgents her unit had been ordered to capture. Rather than chase after them, the unit went after the chief himself. Without him to give the orders, the men made one stupid mistake after another and were quickly rounded up. "Cut off the snake's head," she said, "and the snake will curl up and die."

"Only this snake refuses to die," Mace said. "No matter what law enforcement does, Ronnie Winston's still pulling the strings. It doesn't make a difference that it's from inside prison. And what are the rest of us doing? We're dancing to his tune." Disgust and anger roiled in his voice.

Laurel lifted her chin. "I never was much of a dancer."

Shelley motioned for Mace to hold back as Laurel and Jake filed out of the room. "Laurel has a target on her back. The Collective won't stop coming, and she won't retreat."

Mace watched Shelley, saw the hard swallow of her throat, and knew she was trying to hold back a wave of emotion.

"I'm worried."

He knew the admission didn't come easily to Shelley, who was a warrior in her own right. She had served on a police force before moving to the Secret Service and then to opening her own security firm.

"Her instincts are good." She wouldn't have made the Rangers if she lacked those all-important instincts. Her courage and daring were tempered with an understanding of combat and a fierce resolution to get the job done.

"*Good* isn't good enough," Shelley said. "*Good*

will get you killed. She needs to be elite. Right now, she's not up to full speed."

Mace heard the tremor in Shelley's voice and knew she was referring to the injuries to Laurel's shoulder and arm. So Shelley had noticed them as well and understood the significance. Even a fraction of a second could mean the difference between life and death when it came to responding to a threat.

He thought of the determination in Laurel's eyes, the valiant set of her shoulders.

"She's nothing like I thought," he said, more to himself than to his boss. "What about you? What do you think of her, outside this whole Collective thing?"

"I'm still trying to take it in. A sister we never knew about."

"It's got to be a shock."

"Yeah. I think Laurel's right. I feel it. We have a sister. I never expected that. Victoria—that's what she was going by then—didn't know it, but she gave us a wonderful gift."

Not for the first time, Mace wondered what kind of woman got mixed up in this ugly business, as Laurel's mother had. Then he looked at Shelley, saw the pain in her eyes. The same kind of woman who abandoned her first two children.

"This has got to be hard on you and Jake."

Her curt nod was answer in itself. "I haven't thought of her in years. I thought I was over it, and then this..." Her voice wavered, then firmed. "Whatever brought Laurel here, I'm grateful."

With an effort, Mace pulled himself back to the job. "Laurel will never be safe as long as the Collective has her in its sights." He shook his head in bewilderment and asked the same question they'd all been asking since the beginning. "How does Winston run the Collective from inside a cell?"

"I did some digging on the Collective last night." Shelley pulled out a folder and tapped it. "This is full of people believed to be in its pockets. They range from judges to prosecutors to a couple staffers in the mayor's office. Not to mention police chiefs all the way down to patrol officers."

"In short, we can't trust anyone."

Shelley nodded briefly in acknowledgment. "I'm counting on you to watch her back. I know you well enough to trust you to do just that."

Mace made an embarrassed sound, then sobered. Laurel was family to Shelley, and family meant everything to the woman who had grown up without a loving mother and no father in the picture. "Thanks, boss." He started to leave.

"Mace?"

He stopped, turned.

"Thank you. Jake and I have just found Laurel." His tough-as-nails boss's voice broke, and she averted her eyes. He knew her well enough to know that she was annoyed with herself for showing that emotion. She blew out air through puckered lips and met his gaze once more. "I can't lose her. Not now."

The plea in her voice yanked his heart into a hard knot, and he wanted to give her a brotherly hug. "You won't."

It took two days to set up the visit to see Ronnie Winston. Clearing it with the authorities meant going through several levels of bureaucracy, both inside and outside of the prison. Fortunately, S&J carried some weight in the law enforcement community, and Shelley was able to expedite the process.

Mace still wasn't happy with the agreement to take Laurel to the prison, but he tried to put a positive spin on it. Who knew, maybe her idea to interview Winston in prison would turn up something. All they knew for certain was that he was passing along instructions somehow.

When Mace pulled up to the safe house where a female agent had stayed with Laurel overnight, he wasn't surprised to find Laurel ready early. He'd moved her out of the hotel yesterday—it was too public and exposed.

He got out and opened the door for her.

"Will Sammy be all right?" he asked. "Better to not take him to the prison."

"I've already taken him on a walk this morning. He'll be fine, though he's probably whining right now about being left. He thinks he should go wherever I do."

The heels of her boots kicked up her height another few inches, taking her to eye level with him. She'd dressed in subdued, loose-fitting clothes as he'd instructed, her pants and shirt of olive drab, the color reminding him of Army fatigues. Hair pulled back in a ponytail, her face devoid of makeup, she looked all business. None of her efforts, though, were enough to squash her femininity.

"We have time to pick up something for breakfast on the way."

She shook her head. "After. I want to meet Winston. The sooner we get it over with, the better."

"Have you given any thought as to what you're going to do when all this is over?" He'd thought about it—about her—more than he was comfortable with.

"Sure, I've considered it. A lot. I have six more weeks on medical leave. More, if I push it. The PT guys say that I've made a 'remarkable recovery,' but they're 'cautious' about sending me back to active duty."

"Do you think you'll go back to the Rangers eventually?" He said the words neutrally. He fought the fact that he did have a stake in it, though he'd never admit that to Laurel.

"You know it's not that easy. I've made progress, but my arm is still twitchy. What if I'm out on patrol and some tangos attack? I hesitate a second because I'm afraid that pulling my weapon will set off the pain. One of our guys is gunned down because I'm a second too slow."

"That won't happen."

"I can't be sure that it won't happen. That's the problem. I don't know. I can't know." Frustration rose in her voice.

"I don't see you letting one of your buddies down because you're afraid." Of that he was absolutely certain.

"Thank you for that." She sent him a small smile. "I wouldn't do it consciously. I'm pretty sure about that. But who knows what my subconscious will do?"

She didn't appear to need an answer and spoke little during the rest of the trip, letting him know that the subject was closed.

Mace didn't like taking Laurel to the prison. This was no country club for white-collar criminals. Though it wasn't a supermax prison, the men inside were among the baddest of the bad with rap sheets that would make their own mothers think twice about claiming them. He pulled to the side of the road and turned to Laurel in the truck cab.

"You sure you're up to this? Winston's a snake and twice as mean. It won't matter that you're a woman. He'll do his best to intimidate you, humiliate you, just because he can."

"How did you learn all this about him?"

"I attended several days of his trial, wanted to see what the great and mighty Ronnie Winston was all about."

"What did you come away with?"

"He's a narcissistic sociopath. He'll look at you and you'll want to squirm because you feel dirty being in the same room with him, breathing the same air he does."

"I don't squirm easy."

He ran his gaze over her. "No. I don't guess you do. You don't have to do this. You can walk away. Not just from this visit, but from the whole thing. When you're well enough, you can go back to your unit, put some space between you and the Collective, and let others take it down. This doesn't have to be your fight."

Even as he said the words, he knew Laurel wouldn't do as he suggested. She had guts and grit to spare. She didn't run from a fight, even when it was in her best interest to do so.

Bright color shot into her face. "You think I don't want to walk away? I want to run from it. And because I do, I can't. Not if I ever want to be able to look at myself in the mirror again." She let that sink in. "I'm a Ranger. Just like you."

"You don't have to prove anything to me," he said. "Winston's a sociopath all right, but he's not insane. Not by a long shot. He knows exactly what he's doing and is fully aware of the consequences." Mace ran his gaze over her. "Are you going to be able to face him, knowing that he probably gave the orders to kill your mother?"

"Bernice was never a mother. We shared blood. That was all. Her choice."

"Let's get this over with." He put the truck back in gear and finished driving the short distance to the prison. "Once we're inside, keep your eyes straight ahead. Don't react to anything."

She drew herself up. "I'm no hothouse flower."

"I know. But I'm responsible for you. Do what I say and we'll get through this."

She didn't flinch when she stepped inside the industrial gray walls. She and Mace put their firearms, phones and keys in a locker, along with her jacket. After they were searched and their IDs verified, they were directed to the warden's office.

Warden Dresden greeted them brusquely. He was a beefy man and looked like he could bench press his weight and then some. "I know why you're here. You think Winston's getting messages to the outside. That's nonsense and you're wasting your time." A beat of silence. "And mine. Winston's conversations with visitors are strictly monitored. He doesn't get the orders out that way. Besides, the only person who ever visits him is his wife."

Defensiveness underscored every word. Mace didn't blame the man. They were essentially accusing him of allowing subversive messages to get out of his prison right under his nose.

That said, the warden lifted massive shoulders, his shrug saying that it was no concern of his. "But it's your time to waste. You have thirty minutes with the prisoner. No more." He eyed Laurel critically. "Keep your eyes down. Don't give anyone reason to look at you." He grimaced. "They'll look anyway, but don't give them reason to." He shifted his attention to Mace. "You ought to know better than to bring her here. Isn't like we don't have trouble enough." His shoulders now drooped, the gesture eloquent of weariness with the job.

The warden offered his hand to Laurel. "Follow my instructions and you should be all right." But his voice didn't offer any encouragement. On the contrary, it smacked of doom.

She shook his hand and noticed a green figure on the back of it as the cuff of his shirt shot up. Tattoos weren't uncommon, but she hadn't expected the warden to be sporting ink.

A corrections officer led them to a windowless room where the smell of vomit mixed with cleanser permeated the air and despair hung heavily. The depressing gray walls and ancient flooring added to the effect. "Wait here," the CO instructed and left.

Laurel looked about. "You really know how to show a girl a good time."

Appreciating her humor, Mace nodded. "Yeah. For our next date, maybe we'll visit the town dump. I hear it's a showplace."

"Can't wait."

The small exchange was interrupted when Ronnie Winston was shown in. He wasn't a large man, shouldn't have been intimidating, but there was meanness in his eyes. Meanness and craftiness.

To underestimate him would be a mistake.

EIGHT

Laurel took her time studying Ronnie Winston, comparing the information she'd learned about him with the reality of the man. Winston was in his late forties, though he looked older. The prospect of three consecutive life sentences in a federal pen was enough to age anyone.

But the man led in by a guard with a DOC badge on his uniform didn't look beaten. To the contrary, he appeared confident, his expression one of expectation, despite the fact that his wrists and ankles were chained, attached to another chain around his waist. He shuffled forward, but there was no air of submission in his movements. Rather, he appeared to regard the shackles with amusement, as though he knew a joke no one else did.

The guard pushed Winston to a chair. He sat.

After being shackled to a steel table by the guard, Winston never took his gaze from Laurel. She recognized the intimidation tactic and made no attempt to hide her own scrutiny. The smirk on his face, as though he knew why they were there and was amused by it, emphasized the darkness that emanated from him.

"Ma'am, sir, I'll be on the other side of the door if you need me." With that, the guard departed.

"Nice to have some visitors," Winston said expansively. "Especially such a pretty one." He winked at Laurel.

She did her best not to recoil. She supposed some women might find his oily looks with the slicked-back hair and smarmy smile attractive. She was not among them.

To her, he looked like every other bully she'd ever met, someone who used fear and hatred to intimidate others. She wasn't afraid of him, only repulsed.

"I'd offer my hand, but, as you can see, I'm a little tied up." Winston's smile invited her to join him in the bit of humor.

She didn't.

"I can see this isn't a social call." His air was one of a gracious host extending hospitality. "With whom do I have the honor of meeting?"

"Laurel Landry." She let the words hang for a moment, wanting to see if they had any effect. If Ronnie were calling the shots, he must know the name of the woman he'd sent men to kidnap.

He seemed unfazed. Was his lack of reaction genuine or was he feigning not recognizing her name?

"Mr. Winston, we're here to discuss how you're sending messages to your followers." She didn't see any need to pretend she and Mace were there for any other reason than the truth.

He dropped the bonhomie act, and his smile edged thin. "Wouldn't you like to know?" He spoke quietly, the words evenly spaced, but she sensed the anger simmering just below the surface.

She filed that away. Winston liked to pretend that he wasn't bothered by the circumstances of his incarceration, but he had to be enraged that he was locked up with people he undoubtedly considered his inferiors. From reading Winston's file, she knew he had a narcissistic personality that fed on the belief that he was superior to everyone else.

"As I said, that's why we're here," Laurel continued. "If you help us, it might mean extra time in the yard for you." She understood enough about prisons to know that time in the yard was prized by men like Winston who spent twenty-three out of twenty-four hours per day confined to their cells.

Winston leaned back, ostensibly bored, and tapped his fingers on the table.

She didn't need to look at Mace to feel his reaction to Winston. The air around him was frozen with his anger, his emotions under such rigid control that she was surprised the air didn't crack with it.

Mace would never act unprofessionally, but it was costing him with every second they were in Winston's presence.

Her skin felt slimy. The way Winston had stared at her had laid a chill on her arms.

She shook it off. She was here to get information, not to dwell on the foul energy Winston carried with him. She sucked in a breath, held it. When she finally had to release it, she did so reluctantly.

"You don't even like to breathe the same air as me, do you?"

Winston's taunt flayed her nerves because it was exactly on-target. She could turn her back on the whole thing, return to Afghanistan when she was able, but she wasn't built that way. She had to see this thing through, even if it meant dealing with the likes of Ronnie Winston.

"How'd you know?"

"I'm plenty smart." Bravado oozed with every word. Another wink, and his grin spread fast and fierce.

Maybe she could use that, appeal to his already overinflated ego.

"You're right. You'd have to be smart to run an organization as big as the Southeast Collective."

Winston sneered at her. "I'm smart enough to

know that you're trying to flatter me into telling you how I do it. It won't work."

"Oh?"

"You're out of your league, lady." For the first time since Winston had shuffled into the room, he turned his attention to Mace. "And who are you?"

"Does it matter?"

"Not really. I'm far more interested in the lady." Delighted with himself, Winston let out a donkey bray of a laugh.

Laurel couldn't help the shudder that skipped down her spine. She tried to suppress it, knowing Winston would do his best to use it against her.

Too late. "Got to you, didn't I?"

She hiked up her chin. "Last time I looked, you're the one in shackles. I can walk out of here anytime I like." She caught Mace's infinitesimal nod of approval. Emboldened, she raked her gaze over Winston, letting the insult show. "Maybe you're not so smart after all."

"Smart enough to know that you and the rest of the idiots like you don't have a clue about what's going on."

His smugness was unbelievable. Anger built inside her, threatened to spill over, before she realized that it would get her nowhere.

She wanted to shake the answers from him even while realizing the futility of it. Ronnie Winston was the lowest of life forms, but he wasn't a fool. He was holding on to whatever he knew, waiting for the right time to use it.

"Quit the stalling, Winston," Mace said. "Either give us something or we're out of here." He touched Laurel's elbow when Winston remained silent. "C'mon. He's got nothing we want."

"Don't be too sure." Winston started to wave them back, obviously forgetting that his cuffs were bolted to the table. A look of chagrin passed over his face. "I can tell you stuff. Stuff you want to know." Gone were the cruel taunts and the crueler smile. There was a note of desperation in his voice.

He wanted company, Laurel realized with a start. It didn't matter that they were there to question him, he wanted contact with the outside world, no matter in what form it came.

"I doubt it." Mace stood, then pulled out Laurel's chair.

She jumped up, eager to get away from Winston. She felt dirty simply being in his presence.

"Wait." The word had her stopping, turning.

Laurel held her breath.

"You want to know how I keep running the Collective?" Winston taunted. "The truth? I do it by telepathy." Enjoying his own joke, he laughed heartily.

Laurel realized she'd been taken in by the earnest note of a moment ago. He'd only been toying with them.

Mace shot the man a look so filled with disgust that Laurel shrank under the force of it.

"You're a blight," Mace said. "A blight on everything and everyone you touch." He snapped his fingers. "Oh, that's right. You're a lifer, and once we cut off the orders you're giving, you won't be able to spread your poison ever again."

Winston didn't have a comeback to that but rattled the chains that tethered his hands and feet, rage overtaking him. "You'll be back. You need answers, and I'm the only game in town."

Outside, Laurel inhaled deeply. Even the gray sky, slicked with bloated, darkening clouds, was more appealing than the dank, depressive air of the prison. The rich smells of loam and the nearby river swept through the air. "I feel dirty," she said. "I want to stand under a hot shower for an hour and scrub away the filth."

"When you lie down with pigs, you're bound to get some dirt on you."

She laughed for the first time that morning. "I think you just insulted pigs everywhere."

Mace grinned. "I think you're right. What did you make of him?"

"He's a classic narcissist," she said promptly. "Underappreciated in the world, overappreciated in his own mind. It's imperative that he's looked up to, admired, feared. Without that adulation, he loses his identity."

"You nailed it."

"There's more. He was showing off. Wanted to show us what he could do. Like a little kid saying, 'Look, Mom. See what I did.'"

Mace grimaced. "Why?"

She took her time in answering. "He's arrogant, wants everyone around him to bow to him, to be submissive. It's likely that he requires that in all of his relationships. It's the only way he can feel powerful."

"How do you know all this?"

"I took some profiling classes before being deployed to the Middle East the last time. My commanding officer wanted a few of us to be able to get inside the terrorists' minds." She made a face. "That's the last place I wanted to be, but it paid off. My unit was able to predict where the tangos were going to strike next and capture them."

Mace held the door open for her, and she climbed in the truck. As she buckled her seatbelt, he rounded the truck and climbed in the driver's side.

On impulse, she reached for his hand, letting her fingers skim the hard, callused palm before linking with his.

He lowered his head, pressed his forehead to hers. When his lips found hers, she was ready. Or thought she was.

It was the barest of kisses, hardly more than a caress, but it sent shock waves exploding through her. She'd known a man's kisses before, but they didn't compare to this.

He didn't take, but gave, the kiss unbearably tender. That was the kind of man he was, strong without being hard, gentle without being weak.

When she lifted her head, she blinked at the intensity of senses bombarding her. Colors were brighter, the air sweeter, sounds more vibrant. What was she doing? Rhapsodizing over a kiss outside a prison, its dreary walls only a short distance away.

Only minutes ago, she'd feared she'd never rid her skin of the stench of that horrible room where disinfectant waged a losing battle with despair, but now the air smelled of wildflowers and meadows and mountain streams.

You're losing it, girl.

"What just happened?" Her voice came from a long distance. It didn't sound like hers. She shook her head in a futile attempt to clear it.

"I think it's called a kiss." Mace sounded as shaken as she felt. Good. She didn't want to be the only one whose world had been turned inside out and upside down.

"Yeah. A kiss." Only it wasn't like any kiss she'd ever experienced. Certainly not like the tepid kisses she and Jeffrey had shared.

It had shattered her senses and woven its way into her heart. Whatever the future held for her, she would remember the whisper of startling connection with Mace for the rest of her life. "Something's happening." Had she actually said that aloud? Obviously, she'd lost the little that remained of her mind.

"I know."

"I don't know what to do about it."

"Neither do I."

Laurel felt Mace's gaze on her, the questions plain in his eyes.

She told herself that the kiss was meant to comfort, to remind her that there was goodness in the world, despite the evil spewed by the likes of Ronnie Winston. Mace could not have intended to kiss her there in the shadow of the prison.

Something long-buried inside of her threatened to break free.

She had spent most of her adult life serving her country. The rigorous mental and physical training she'd undergone as a Ranger had taught her to channel her emotions. Giving in to them now wasn't in her game plan. Still, she was curious. Curious and more than a little afraid of the feelings welling up within her.

"Do you want to talk about it?"

"I was out of line," he said evenly.

His assertion sent a shaft of pain through her, nearly causing her to tell him that she wanted to explore what had just taken place. But she couldn't. Because she didn't know.

Mace started the ignition, exited the prison grounds, and pulled into the road's sparse traffic.

Until learning of Bernice's murder, she had had her life laid out in a straight trajectory. Join the Army and then make Rangers. Her injury had temporarily derailed her, but she'd power through the remainder of rehab and return to what she'd spent her whole life preparing for.

Lately, though, questions kept popping up. Shelley had ordered DNA tests for herself, Jake and Laurel. What if she was totally wrong in her assumption that she was related to Jake and Shelley? And then there was the question of what had happened when Mace had kissed her.

She wasn't given time to ponder it, for at that moment, a muscular-looking pickup truck raced toward them. The growl of the engine promised that this was no ordinary truck but one that had been hopped up for maximum power.

Mace swerved, managed to avoid a crash, but the pickup reversed and came at them again. There was nowhere to go. A deafening crash later, one of their wheels slid on the embankment. He slammed on the brakes, but it wasn't enough to keep the truck from going over.

Seconds later, it was plunging into the river.

NINE

Laurel struggled to unhook the seat belt, but it held fast. She tugged, yanked, pulled, but nothing freed the buckle from its latch. Mace had quickly undone his seat belt. Why wouldn't hers budge?

Seeing her predicament, he pulled a knife from his boot and worked to cut through the seat belt, but the pressure of the water worked against the effort, and he couldn't get any traction. The truck wasn't fully submerged—yet.

She motioned for him to go. No sense in both of them dying. The water was quickly rising in the cab of the truck. Too quickly.

She was trapped.

She knew it, just as he did. Once more she gestured for him to leave her, and he shook his head.

Water filled the cab. Mace couldn't breathe underwater any more than she could. Without oxygen to their brains, they would die.

He had to leave. Now.

Just when she thought it was all over for both of them, the seat belt gave way under Mace's persistent sawing with the knife. He kicked the door open.

Laurel pushed with her legs, and started to swim toward the surface, aware every moment that Mace was right behind her. He'd saved her life. Again.

Grateful to be alive, she stumbled out of the water. Drenched clothes dragged at her, slowing her progress. A relieved sigh never made it past her lips. Two goons were waiting for her and Mace on the shore. They must have been watching and seen that she and Mace had made it out of the river.

"We got this," Mace said.

She gave him a thumbs-up and zeroed in on one of the men.

Both men were the size of small mountains. Not a problem. Their size could make them slow, but first she and Mace had to disarm them.

"So you're the little girl playing Ranger." Her opponent moved closer as he pulled a Glock on her.

"I'm the woman who earned her Ranger badge."

His gaze raked her. "You're mighty skinny to be out playing war with men."

"I don't play at anything." Thinking of the M4s and M24 SAWs she'd employed in Afghanistan, she added, "Especially war." Right now, she was wishing she had one or both of those bad boys at the ready. Even her much smaller Sig would have been useful, but it had been lost in the river.

"Seems you have something that belongs to some friends of ours and they want it back. Come along with us and save us all some trouble. No sense in making it harder on yourself." Contempt rolled through his voice and the sneer on his ugly face.

"No sense in giving in, either, and making it easier on you. Where'd the Collective find a dirtbag like you anyway?"

The man's lips drew in a hard line, but he said, pleasantly enough, "Why'd you want to go and say something like that? Just when we were getting along so well."

"I failed my course at Emily Post." With that, she kicked the gun from his hand, earning a growl.

Laurel then speared her foot into his gut.

He grunted but didn't fall. He was built like a redwood and wouldn't topple easily. She gritted her teeth. She was in for a fight.

He advanced, huge arms dangling from powerful shoulders. She danced back. Though she didn't have brawn, she did have the best training the United States Army could provide. More, she had a powerful will to survive.

She judged her opponent and her opening. She couldn't match him for strength. On the other hand, she had agility on her side. Agility and determination.

When he threw himself at her, she dodged, allowing the weight of his body to carry him forward so that he fell flat on his face. He picked himself up and scowled at her. The hatred in his eyes promised that he'd make her regret humiliating him.

Training had her broadening her stance, planting her feet more firmly on the uneven ground. *Choose your spot.* Her Ranger instructor's words echoed in her mind. She was making a stand.

She only hoped it wouldn't be her last.

"Pretty fancy footwork," he said between clenched teeth.

The gleam in her opponent's eyes was that of a big cat, toying with his prey, knowing he had the advantage. He sprang again, and though she blocked the blow with her arm, she felt the force of it zing through her body, explode into her injured shoulder.

Agony flooded through her, so intense that she feared she might pass out. She held on to consciousness by sheer force of will.

The second blow came on the heels of the first and sent her sprawling to the muddy riverbank. He was on her, pummeling her with fists the size of country hams.

Laurel rolled free of her captor, got to her feet and assumed a fighting crouch. He mirrored her actions, but still, she was able to jab her fist into his midsection. Though she dodged his blows the best she could, she couldn't escape all of them. They came too fast, punishing in their force.

Anger surged inside her, and she hardened it into pure resolve. Somehow the Collective had known that she and Mace had planned to visit Winston today and had staged this ambush. Someone had betrayed them.

With strength she didn't know she possessed, she flipped him over, then placed her knee at the small of his back, anchoring him in place. But he wasn't done with her and reared back, his head slamming her in the face.

Stunned by the blow, she toppled backward. Spears of light streaked across her vision, and she tasted blood.

Her opponent growled something low in his throat as he got to his feet. When he pulled a knife from the scabbard at his side, she crab-crawled backward. The knife, military issue, gleamed with deadly purpose. It arced toward her. At the last moment, she rolled, catching him off guard.

"You're done for," he said.

"Not by a long shot."

She rolled again, and, as he moved in, kicked

out with her right leg, aiming for his face. Her foot connected with his nose.

Blood spurted down his mouth and chin onto his neck. He pressed the palm of his hand to his nose. "You broke it." He let loose a war cry.

She reveled in it for a moment, but only a moment. The rage in his eyes warned her that if he got his hands on her, he'd enjoy inflicting as much pain as possible. Blood continued to stream down his face.

He swiped a meaty hand across his cheek, scowling when it came away smeared with blood. "Guess I'm gonna have to make sure you're sorry for that." He paused. "Real sorry. Sure hate to mess up that pretty face of yourn."

"I'll take care of my face. You take care of yourn."

He'd obviously sensed that he'd been mocked. "We'll see how pretty you are when this is all over." In a blind rage, he accidentally dropped his knife.

She made a grab for it, snatching it away before he realized what had happened, got to her feet and closed the small distance between them. She put the knife to his throat. "Tell me who sent you. I want a name."

"No way. They'll kill me."

She nicked his skin with the knife. "I'll kill you if you don't." She didn't intend on killing him, only scaring him into giving her the information she needed.

But she didn't have the opportunity to work on the man, as his partner signaled him. Her opponent twisted out of her grasp and ran to the truck parked on the side of the road.

Exhilaration poured through her, and riding on an adrenaline-filled high, she fist bumped Mace. "We did it. We sent them running with their tails between their legs."

"Don't be so sure," he said, pointing to the road where the two men were grabbing extra guns from their truck.

"What are they waiting for?"

"My guess? Reinforcements."

Not intending on waiting around to see if he was right, Mace grabbed Laurel's hand. "We've got to get out of here. Now."

She didn't ask questions, only gripped his hand harder and ran.

The Georgia forest was thickly wooded. The woods rioted with color as summer waned to autumn, but none of that mattered. Armed men were coming after them with a two-pronged intent: to kill him and take Laurel.

The deeper they plunged into the forest, the darker it grew. A slice of sunlight found its way through the dense forest, casting misshapen shadows on the ground. He noticed Laurel shivering. What he wouldn't give for the tactical gear he'd routinely carried on Ranger missions.

They jumped over roots big around as his arm, rotted trees, and vines snaking over the forest bed.

Laurel stumbled over a root and went down hard.

He helped her up. "You okay?"

"Fine."

But he noticed her pace had slowed as she favored her left ankle. He had to hand it to her. She didn't complain. Not once. She just kept going.

Every few minutes Mace listened, trying to catch any sound of the pursuers behind them. Maybe they had lost them.

Though Laurel had kept up a steady pace, he noticed she was slowing down with every step now. That ankle needed to be iced, wrapped, and her leg elevated. It was up to him to get them out of the woods and to a safe place.

He stopped. Listened. "Do you hear it?"

"What?" Alarm sounded in her voice.

"Nothing. I think we lost them."

"Good." She sank down against a tree, leaned back.

It was then he noticed the lines bracketing her mouth. She was obviously in more pain than he'd realized.

He hunkered down beside her. "May I?" He gestured to her ankle.

"Sure." A groan punctuated her words.

After taking off her boot and sock, he examined the ankle. It didn't appear to be broken, only sprained, but a sprain could cause a world of hurt. He cut a sleeve from his shirt, wrapped her ankle as tightly as possible and then slipped the sock and boot back on her foot. "That will have to hold for now."

The screeching of birds and rustling of branches told him he and Laurel were no longer alone. The pounding of feet confirmed it. He paused, listened for a minute. By his estimation, four—or more—tangos were on his and Laurel's tail. "They're back, and they're getting closer."

Mace calculated the odds of outrunning their pursuers. Not good. If the men had any military training at all, they'd know to split up and flank him and Laurel. In addition, they were already winded from their struggle in the river. "We can't outrun them."

"What do we do?" There was no panic in her voice, and he gave her props for that.

"We outthink them." Mace pointed to a culvert he'd spotted. "Ready to get dirty?"

"Ready as I'll ever be."

They moved to the edge, and he counted aloud to three. "Jump!"

TEN

Along with Mace, Laurel jumped, ending in a roll down the steep side of the culvert, collecting leaves and debris as she went. She kept her arms crossed over her chest as she rolled. At last, she came to a stop, ending up in murky water and mud. Would it be enough to conceal her and Mace?

She held her breath and prayed.

Above, she heard the pounding of running footsteps. When the sound of the footfalls grew faint and then disappeared completely, she allowed herself to believe Mace's ruse had worked. Still, neither she nor Mace moved. Not yet.

"We're clear," he said.

With a whoosh, she released her breath in a slow exhale. With Mace's arm to steady her, she stood, then gave a grimace of disgust. Mud clung to almost every inch of her, including her eyelashes. She swiped at her eyes with the back of her hand, only to discover that she'd succeeded in smearing more mud onto her face.

Something stung her neck. Again. Mosquitos. Great. Now she'd have welts in addition to being covered with mud and muck from head to toe.

Mace helped her up the bank on the other side of the culvert and, after looking her over, gave a mock salute. "Very fetching, Ranger Landry."

"Same to you." She looked down at her clothes. "No way will we be able to hitch a ride looking like this."

"Depends on the ride."

They made their way to the road.

Mace had been right. A sedan passed without the driver giving them as much as a glance. Then a battered pickup slowed and pulled to a stop.

A man who could have been anywhere between forty and eighty stuck his head out the window. "You folks need a lift?"

Mace grinned. "Sure do."

"Well, then, climb on in." The man hitched his thumb toward the back of the truck.

Laurel rounded the truck and burst out laughing. "It's perfect."

She climbed in and plunked down in a corner. Two pigs, which she decided were sows after a quick look, were in the bed of the truck.

Mace joined her. "Might as well make ourselves comfortable," he said and stretched out his legs.

"Do you think we lost them?" she asked, referring to the tangos.

"For now."

"You're loving this, aren't you?"

He grinned at her. "And you aren't?"

"Yeah. I guess I am."

In the last two hours, she'd met the murderous head of the Collective's Southeast region, fought off two men intent on killing Mace and abducting her, and had made a wild run through the forest that ended up with her in a culvert covered with mud and muck. Enjoying a respite from all that, plus the company of two friendly-looking sows, was definitely a step-up.

"You're beautiful."

Her heart stopped, then did a fluttery dance in her chest before settling.

"You beat everything. You wait until I'm covered in mud and mosquito bites and then decide to tell me that I'm beautiful."

"Because you are." His voice dropped, and he leaned in. The kiss was long and slow. If she had been standing, her knees would have gone weak. She'd always dismissed the saying as a cliché, but now she understood. As it was, the kiss had turned her mind to mush, and she struggled to regain her equilibrium.

Easy, girl, she cautioned herself, with a reminder that the kiss was only a reaction to the danger they'd shared a short while ago, a confirmation that they were alive.

Despite her warning, though, she couldn't help but respond to the gentle pressure of his lips.

He cupped the back of her neck and let his forehead rest against hers before pulling away. "You're some kind of strong."

"Because I didn't faint at the idea of sharing a ride with two pigs?" Her tart words couldn't mask the exhaustion in her voice.

"Because you just keep going. No matter what." He didn't give her time to chew over that, instead gesturing to her ankle. "How's it doing?"

"Not bad. It helped when you strapped it up."

When she caught a whiff of something foul, she started to attribute it to the pigs, then realized that the smell came from her. "I'm afraid they smell better than we do."

Mace grinned. "I'm thinking you're right." His expression turned serious. "Those men were waiting for us. It was no coincidence that they knew we'd be coming out of the prison at that time."

"We're on the same page there. Someone had to alert them to where we'd be."

"Someone in the prison."

"You said the Collective had a long reach," Laurel said. "This proves it. And we can't do anything about it. We don't know who in the police is on the take. And if we do report this, they'll say that without proof, their hands are tied. Who do we trust?"

"Ourselves. Ourselves and S&J."

The sobering exchange reminded her that they had a long way to go before they could put an end to Winston's reign of terror.

He reached out to chuck her under the chin. "You and I have some things to figure out once this is all over. Maybe we will. Maybe we won't. In the meantime, we'd better keep things just business between us."

Business? Her brain agreed. But her heart? Her heart had its own needs, and business was not one of them. And what of the kiss he'd just given her? She looked at him in exasperation and then gave up trying to make sense of the whole thing.

The obliging driver dropped them not far from the safe house. "When I tell my missus about this, she'll likely say some prayers for you folks. Looks like you could use 'em."

Mace helped Laurel down from the truck.

She turned to the driver. "Thank you. And thank your missus for us, too."

Attracting odd stares, and, in some cases, horrified looks by pedestrians, they hoofed it to the safe house.

After they cleaned up, Mace checked her ankle and rewrapped it, using an elastic bandage this time.

Mace handed her a Sig Sauer, similar to her

own that had been lost. "Don't worry," he said. "It's registered."

"Thank you."

She saw to Sammy, and a quick lunch later, they took a cab to S&J headquarters where they found both Shelley and Jake in her office.

Before Laurel and Mace could report on the meeting with Winston and the ambush, Shelley said, "Cheek swab time." She gave Laurel a cotton swab. "Easy-peasy," Shelley said. "Jake and I have already done ours."

Jake looked on, expression unreadable, but he didn't voice any objection.

Laurel swabbed her cheek, then placed the swab in a small plastic bag that came with the kit. A myriad of emotions swirled through her, but hope was at the center as she acknowledged to herself how much she wanted the test to prove that she was, indeed, Shelley and Jake's sister.

"Thank you," she said simply. Aware of the huskiness of her voice, she cleared her throat and gestured to Mace. "It's time to 'fess up and tell them about the truck and the rest of our day."

Shelley pretended to scowl when she learned about the truck. "You go through vehicles faster than Chloe does diapers," she said to Mace. "Good thing we're insured." She excused herself, then returned several minutes later.

"We're rattling somebody's cage," Mace said.

"And they're rattling ours right back." Laurel pushed a stray strand of hair back from her face.

"How'd they know you'd be at the prison?" Shelley asked. "It wasn't a coincidence that they found you."

Mace shook his head. "You're right. It was no coincidence. Someone knew. You made the arrangements for the visit two days ago, right?"

Shelley nodded.

"Who did you talk to?"

"The assistant chief at the bureau of prison affairs and, after that, the warden." Her brow furrowed. "Either of them could be on the Collective's payroll. Maybe that's how Winston's getting word out of the prison."

"Other people had to know as well," Laurel said. "Secretaries. The deputy warden. The guard that brought Winston to us. Word that we were planning on visiting him could have gotten out any number of ways."

"I can run background checks on them," Shelley said. "See who might have a big need of money."

Jake barked out a laugh. "Who doesn't?"

"I hear you," Mace said. "Still, we've got to start somewhere." He shifted to Laurel. "Are you okay? We've had what some might call a full day."

That elicited a laugh from all four of them.

"I'm as okay as I can be, considering. It's not

every day that I get to ride in the back of a truck with two pigs."

Shelley leaned closer. "Now this I've got to hear."

Mace's mind might have been on the discussion going on around him about pigs, mud and who could have set up him and Laurel outside the prison. It might have been, probably should have been, but it wasn't.

Instead, it was far removed from the topic, his thoughts centering on Laurel and the kisses they'd shared this morning outside the prison and in the farmer's truck. The memory of both still lingered on his lips and in his mind.

The direction of his thoughts left him edgy. Smarter to put that aside, as there were other things—bigger things—to feel edgy about. Like the Collective's unrelenting pursuit of Laurel and what it would do to her once it got its hands on the ledger.

His lips tightened at the mere idea of something happening to her.

Laurel was quickly becoming important to him. Too important?

It wasn't difficult to find reasons to admire her. Courage, honor and determination to do the right thing were as much a part of her as were her chestnut hair, golden eyes and freckles. She wasn't one to run from a fight but would draw a line in the sand and then dare anyone to cross it.

The quiet goodness that colored everything Laurel did drew him to her as much as did her undeniable beauty of which she seemed totally unaware. Another of her charms.

Aside from the integrity she wore so effortlessly, her faith also set her apart. He took a step back from his thoughts. Though she hadn't said so, her belief would always be a stumbling block between them if they were ever to have a relationship.

A second step back. No need to worry about her faith or his lack of the same. A relationship—with Laurel or anyone for that matter—wasn't in the future for him.

But a man could dream, couldn't he?

His meanderings annoyed him. He was an ex-Ranger, one who had seen too much of the world's ugliness. He had no business thinking of Laurel as anything more than a client, a very appealing, very attractive client, but a client all the same.

Neutrality was a far better position. He let his gaze rest on Laurel and forgot about any neutrality in his feelings for her.

Get over it, man. Laurel will return to the Rangers. You'll stay here and keep working for S&J. That's the way you want it.

"Mace, you with us?" Jake asked.

Mace looked up, hoping guilt that he had blanked out the discussion for a few minutes didn't show in his eyes. "Yeah. Right here."

When the talk ended, Jake hung back after Shelley and Laurel left. "Mace, got a minute?"

Pretty sure where this was going, Mace nodded.

Jake leaned back against Shelley's desk. "You like Laurel. In fact, I'd say that you more than like her."

Mace didn't like where this was going. "Is that a problem?" Forgotten was his lecture to himself that Laurel was only a client.

"You're one of the best operatives S&J has. What's more, you're one of the best men I know. You'd never deliberately hurt Laurel, but you might end up hurting her anyway."

Mace wanted to deny it but held his tongue. "What do you want me to do?"

"I want you to think about where this thing with Laurel is going." Jake slanted a hard look Mace's way. "I know you care about her."

Mace kept his voice even. "Like you said, I care about her." Caring was okay. He cared about other people, including Jake and Shelley and their families.

Jake stood, paced the confines of his sister's office. "I make it a practice to stay out of other people's business, but Laurel might be family.

Shelley sure seems to think so. And that makes it my business."

"Laurel's a Ranger. Seems to me that she can take care of herself."

"Ordinarily, yes, but she's also vulnerable. Not just because of her injury. All this stuff with her maybe being our half-sister complicates things."

Mace nodded.

Logic and reason had ruled his life ever since he could remember. With Laurel, that had all ended. He had allowed his feelings to gain the upper hand. He thought of the sigh of pleasure she'd issued after he'd kissed her in the back of the farmer's truck. It was soft as a baby's whisper, as powerful as the feelings that shimmered between them.

He should have been focused on the mission—protecting her from the Collective—rather than fantasizing over her, but he was off his game and had been ever since meeting Laurel.

Maybe he was overthinking the whole thing. Laurel was an assignment. As long as they were working together, he'd enjoy her company. No biggie.

Yeah, right.

ELEVEN

"Come to dinner tonight," Shelley said as Mace caught up to her and Laurel as they headed to the parking lot. "Both of you."

"I've got to get back to Sammy," Laurel said. "I've left him alone for too long today."

"Bring him along."

"We've got no wheels," Mace reminded Shelley. He noted the tiredness in Laurel's eyes and that she was favoring her injured ankle again. Instinctively, he tucked an arm around her waist.

A flicker of Shelley's eyes said that she'd caught the gesture, but she didn't say anything regarding it. "Yes, you do. I ordered a rental, another rental," she emphasized, "when you told me about the truck. It's here waiting for you. Try to make it last more than a day." Her grin took any sting out of the words. "Dinner's at seven, all right?"

Laurel looked to Mace, who nodded. They swung by the safe house to pick up Sammy. The dog greeted them joyfully and, after she saw to his needs, climbed into the truck.

She was quiet on the drive to Shelley and Caleb's house, too intent on thinking of the interview with Ronnie Winston to make conversation. He didn't impress her as someone with the intelligence and initiative she'd expect of the head of the Southeast Collective.

When they arrived, Laurel felt that she'd stepped into a different world from that in which she'd grown up.

Love filled the house. It was there in the scatter of toys, in the flowers that spilled out of a fat vase, in the family photos that covered nearly every flat surface.

"Will the children be all right with Sammy? He's a sweetheart, but he's a big dog. I wouldn't want him to frighten them."

"Why don't we let Tommy answer that?" Shelley called Tommy from the other room. "We've got company."

Tommy ran into the room and skidded to a stop. "Ah, Shelley. I was just…"

Whatever he'd been about to say took a back seat to Sammy, who sat patiently at Laurel's side.

"What a great dog. Is he yours?" Tommy hunkered down to pet Sammy, who gave a rumble of pleasure at having his neck scratched.

Tommy looked to be about nine years old. The

patches on his jeans and the scrape on his elbow had Laurel smiling.

"Tommy, this is Laurel and Sammy. You know Mace. How would you feel about taking Sammy out back to play?"

Tommy turned to Laurel. "Can I?"

"He'd love it."

"What about his leg?" Concern creased a line between his brows.

"Sammy's learned to compensate. He'll keep up with you just fine."

"Come on, Sammy," Tommy said, getting to his feet.

After a look at Laurel, Sammy took off after Tommy, who whooped with delight.

The four adults looked after boy and dog. "Love at first sight," Shelley said.

Laurel smiled. "That's the way it was for me when I first saw Sammy."

"What happened to him, if you don't mind me asking."

"Sammy was an explosives-sniffing dog. He went into a school, alerted his handlers. They cleared the school, but missed one of the bombs. Sammy didn't get out in time, along with me and three others. The doctors operated but couldn't save his leg. He was decommissioned, around the same time I was put on medical leave. He's a hero, as much as any soldier who's served." With an effort, she kept her voice steady.

"What will you do with him when you return to duty?"

"I don't know," Laurel admitted. "He and I... we're family."

"He's fortunate to have you."

"It's the other way around. I'm the fortunate one. Sammy was there for me when I needed him." That was the truth. Without Sammy, Laurel wasn't certain she'd have had the courage to get up every day and endure the torment through which the physical therapist put her.

Shelley's eyes turned soft. "I'd say you were there for each other. That's what family does."

Laurel heard the love in Shelley's voice.

"Let's go outside." Shelley flung open the French doors at the side of the room, gestured to the garden which boasted a small courtyard surrounded by plants and flowers of every shape and color. Comfortable-looking lawn chairs and lounges invited you to sit down and put up your feet, while a cedar bench cozied up against a backdrop of greenery.

While Caleb took Mace to the far side of the garden to look at a project, Shelley and Laurel sat on a wicker bench.

Laurel stared in wonder at a garden dusted with nature's beauty.

Ambitious clematis, too restless to stay put, climbed a pergola, purple flowers the size of saucers blooming in celebration of the earth's bounty. Wisteria quietly found purchase on the handles of an ancient wheelbarrow where delicate violas happily shared space with hearty marigolds. Woodland faeries fashioned from intricately carved cypress played hide-and-seek in the jungle of flowers.

Shelley picked up one of the faeries and ran her fingers over it. "Caleb made this one when Tommy's adoption was final." She set the faerie down and picked up another. "And this when Chloe was born."

Laurel made a slow turn. Strings of miniature lights wound their way through a wrought iron arbor. White lights twinkled against the night, a sprinkling of diamond dust.

The effect was at once wild and oddly restful.

She made a sound of pleasure. The garden, redolent with the scent of rich earth, magnolias and roses, promised a return to earlier times, when gracious living and gentility were the norm and a slower way of life was not only accepted but expected, a time of handwritten notes on engraved stationery and freshly squeezed lemonade with sprigs of mint served in frosted glasses.

The garden was really an extension of the indoors. The eclectic theme of the living room was continued here with mismatched pieces married together in a cheerful mix that was both soothing and energizing. A vintage sundial kept time next to a group of three iron balls that looked like a child's toys, only they were giant sized. As if there weren't enough blooms growing in a riot of colors and scents, pots of flowers were placed in random spots, including climbing the rungs of an ancient ladder.

"It's beautiful," Laurel said honestly.

"It's home." Shelley spread her arms to encompass the whole. "This place was all I could afford when I decided I wanted a house of my own. Now I couldn't think of living anywhere else. Caleb and Tommy helped with the garden. Turns out they have the green thumbs of the family." She gave a rueful glance at her own hands. "Whereas I've been known to kill a silk plant."

"You've made it your own. All of it. You and Caleb and Tommy and Chloe."

Shelley smiled, obviously pleased. "We have. We're not a traditional family, but tradition's overrated. We are what we make ourselves and what the Lord makes of us."

"You've made something good here. Wonderful and good." Laurel kept her voice neutral, but an old wistfulness whispered through her. With an effort, she held herself back from hoping too hard that she might someday have a place with them.

Home isn't where you go, she thought, recalling something she'd read on the back of a cereal box years ago. *It's where you come back to.*

Shelley and Caleb had done that here. They'd

made a home with toys and flowers and the sounds of children's voices. Laurel had never known the love of family. The closest thing she'd ever had to a family was the barracks where she'd done basic training. She pushed away that depressing thought.

She told herself that she liked being unencumbered by possessions and other people's feelings, but the truth was she wanted ties, wanted the love and mess and noise that came with family.

Suck it up, girl.

"I knew I wanted a home," Shelley said. "A real one where I could be a mother to Tommy and Chloe. Neither of us—" she sent an understanding look Laurel's way "—had much of an example in Bernice, or Victoria as she was then, but I learned. Poor Tommy. He had to put up with my first attempts at mothering, but he survived."

Laurel knew that Shelley was speaking of more than Tommy surviving her mothering. In researching S&J and Shelley and Jake in particular, she'd learned that Tommy's parents had been murdered, and he, along with Caleb and Shelley, had become the targets of killers who had no remorse. Protecting Tommy had brought Caleb and Shelley together.

"It's obvious that you love him and that he loves you."

"I can't imagine my life without Caleb, Tommy and Chloe." Shelley's eyes glistened with tears.

"I'm sorry," she said huskily with a quick swipe of her thumbs to wipe away the tears. "Every time I think about what the Lord's given me, the waterworks start. What about you? Do you think you'll marry someday, start a family?"

Laurel took her time in answering. "I don't know," she said at last. Despite her longing for a real home, she'd never thought of herself as a wife, a mother. Her career in the Rangers was everything to her. Or it had been. Her future loomed uncertainly. If her shoulder didn't heal, there'd be no career to go back to.

"I don't know how to be a mother," Laurel confessed. "Or if I even want to. What if I mess up and my child suffers because of it?"

Shelley nodded. "Bernice did a number on all of us. If you want to talk about it, I'm a good listener."

Laurel stared down at her hands as though they held the answers to questions that had plagued her for as long as she could remember. Did she dare take Shelley up on her invitation to talk about what they had both suffered at the hands of the woman who had given birth to them but had never been a mother?

Bernice had abandoned both Jake and Shelley. In Laurel's case, Bernice hadn't as much abandoned her as made it such that Laurel, who had just turned sixteen, had had no choice but to leave. It was that or fall prey to the dealers and lowlifes who had frequented Bernice's trailer on a regular basis.

Laurel raised her head to gaze at the sister who looked nothing like her. What did they have in common but shared pain, a pain they had each thought was theirs alone? Did that make it better? Or worse?

"I know," Shelley said, reading Laurel's mind with ease. "We don't look a thing alike. I'm ridiculously short while you're—"

"Ridiculously tall."

"I was going to say you're tall and beautiful. You could have been a model. Ever think of it?"

Laurel shuddered. "No. Having people stare at me, take pictures of me like I'm a thing rather than a person. No."

Shelley grinned. "I get it." Her smile winked out. "I guess you had enough of that when you made Rangers."

Finally. Someone who understood. "Sometimes I felt like I was on display 24/7." Another shudder. "One of the photographers even suggested I put on makeup. Like I'd be wearing makeup tramping through the mountains or crawling through the desert."

"Idiot."

In perfect harmony, they smiled at each other. The smiles died when both women acknowledged that wasn't what Laurel wanted to talk about.

Laurel drew a deep breath. "You and Jake

made it through everything she did to you and came out on top." There was no need to identify who the "she" was.

"And so will you."

"I'm not so sure. Sometimes I still ask myself why she couldn't love me and if it was my fault. I know it's foolish, but—"

"She couldn't love anyone," Shelley cut in. "That's on her. Not on you."

Laurel prayed with everything in her that Shelley was right.

After the day he and Laurel had put in, the last thing Mace had wanted to do was go to dinner tonight. He'd longed for a quiet night with a good book, a bowl of ice cream and maybe some jazz playing in the background. Now that he was here, though, he was glad he'd agreed.

Shelley and Caleb's home was beautiful, not because of the appointments or furnishings but because of the love that filled the space. He liked the bits and pieces of everyday living that were strewn about. He liked that Shelley made no attempt to apologize for the clutter. He liked the small touches that said this was a home, not a showplace.

When Caleb excused himself to start the steaks, Mace wandered back to where Laurel and Shelley sat and unabashedly listened to them talk about the mother who had never been a mother.

He knew Shelley and Jake's story, and now he was learning more of Laurel's. His lips stitched closed in anger at the woman who had essentially abandoned her children, leaving them to fend on their own. Even though it had been Laurel who'd done the leaving, she'd done so out of self-preservation.

His childhood hadn't been perfect, but at least he'd known that his parents loved him. Shelley and Jake had had each other, but Laurel had had no one. She'd made something of herself and had done it on her own. From what he could see, she had done a fine job.

Caleb reappeared, took a look at Mace and said, "Listen to them. They sound like they grew up with each other."

Mace had met Caleb Judd only a few years ago but had quickly come to regard him as a good friend.

"I never understood how hard it must have been on Jake and Shelley and now Laurel with the mother they had."

Caleb clenched his hand, unclenched it and clenched it again. "Yeah. Shelley still keeps parts of her childhood from me. She thinks it'll make me sad. What it mostly does is make me angry. Sometimes I'll hear her crying in her sleep. I'll wake her and ask her what's wrong. She never says much, but I can see the pain in her eyes. I've never felt more helpless."

Mace had entertained the same feelings. "Why would a woman who clearly disliked her children keep them for as long as she did? Why not give them up to the state where they might be raised in foster homes or even put up for adoption? Why not give them the opportunity to be loved?"

"Selfishness," Caleb answered promptly. "She didn't want them, but she didn't want anyone else to have them either. And then there's the money thing."

It made a horrible kind of sense. Laurel was too smart not to have known. What must it have done to a young girl to know that the only reason her mother kept her around was for money?

Caleb took out his cell. "Mind if I turn on the news for a minute?"

"Not at all."

Caleb brought up the news on the phone just as the anchorman was giving a rundown of the day's events.

"At the bottom of the hour, we've learned that local man Tony Wexler was found dead in an alley. Police reports reveal that his throat had been cut…"

Mace inhaled sharply as a picture of his snitch was shown.

Tony the Snitch had been murdered. And Mace had been the cause.

"I'm glad we found each other," Shelley said to Laurel. "The DNA test hasn't come through yet, but I know. Here." She placed a hand on her heart.

"So am I." Laurel covered her own heart, rejoicing in the knowledge she might have a sister. "I'm a Ranger, but in some ways I'm still that little girl wanting her mother to love her. Does it ever go away?"

The warm understanding in Shelley's eyes was balm to the ragged edges of Laurel's heart. "With the Lord's help."

With the Lord's help. Laurel held on to those words.

"I'm sorry you were alone," Shelley said. "I had Jake. He looked out for me."

"I survived. I got my GED when I was sixteen, left home, and never looked back." No, she thought, in a moment of self-honesty, that wasn't true. She'd sometimes wondered if Bernice had noticed that her child was no longer there or if it had been business as usual. "I hadn't spoken to Bernice in more than a decade."

"And then you got the call that she'd been murdered."

It shamed Laurel that she'd considered, even for a moment, not returning for the funeral.

Bernice had never been a mother, but a sense of duty had sent Laurel back to that Podunk town with its harsh judgments that had been meted out to anyone who didn't measure up to the narrow-minded standards, especially to anyone who lived in the trailer park that was on the wrong side of the tracks.

Whatever Bernice had or hadn't been, she hadn't deserved to be murdered in her own home.

Laurel looked about the pretty garden that was really an extension of the house and once more wished she'd known this kind of home, where small bits and pieces of daily living mixed together in chaotic harmony.

The love for family shone everywhere she looked. In the basket of toys flanking a chair. In the football that rested on a table, an incongruous note against a pot of African violets.

Caleb and Mace joined them then, with Caleb slipping an arm around Shelley's shoulders.

"You gave me family I didn't know I had," Shelley said and reached for Laurel's hand, gave it a gentle squeeze before releasing it. "I should be thanking you."

Laurel bit down on her lip. She would not cry. She would not cry. She would not cry.

She started to stand, winced and prayed that neither Shelley nor Caleb had noticed. Mace already knew about the IED. She dug her teeth into her lip once more to steady herself. A spasm ran through her right arm up to her shoulder. This time she couldn't control the flinch.

"Your arm's giving you trouble, isn't it?" Caleb asked. He rounded the chair and offered her a hand up. "I noticed it right away. Doing PT for it?"

A grimace took hold on her mouth as she thought of the hours of grueling physical therapy. So much for working to downplay her injury. "I was. Before…before Bernice and everything."

"I'm guessing you took shrapnel to the shoulder and it shattered some bone. Now it's messing up your arm."

"Something like that. How did you know?"

"I had a buddy who went through the same thing."

She asked the question and wasn't sure she wanted the answer. "Did he make it back?" What would she do if she couldn't be a Ranger any longer? Up until now, she had refused to think that she wouldn't be able to return to the work she had trained for most of her adult life.

"No." Caleb didn't soft-pedal his answer, and, for that, she was grateful. She didn't need well-intentioned platitudes. She needed honesty. "He's working for a private firm now. He's doing well enough, considering."

"You never complain," Shelley said.

Laurel squared her shoulders. "Whining doesn't

help." She'd never been a whiner. She wasn't about to start now.

"It's not whining when it's family." Shelley rose as well and tenderly hugged Laurel, careful of her arm. "We'll see this through together. All of it. If you need to set up PT here, Jake and I can help." A frown gathered in her eyes. "Jake's had his share of therapy for his leg. He knows the ins and outs of the system."

The tears came then. Despite everything Laurel could do to stop them, they trickled down her cheeks.

Mace didn't say anything, only handed her a handkerchief.

"Thank you," she murmured, then turned back to Shelley and Caleb. "I don't know what to say. To either of you. You had no reason to accept me, but you did."

Shelley squeezed Laurel's good arm. "Say that you'll let us help you."

Laurel hugged her sister back, and, after a moment's hesitation, awkwardly did the same with Caleb.

One corner of his mouth twitched in a smile. "I always wanted a sister. Looks like I've got one now."

What would Mace say if she were to hug him just then? Would he understand that the hug she gave him would be far different than the one she'd just shared with Caleb?

Shelley called Tommy to wash up. She got Chloe up from her nap and brought her out to join the party.

The four adults, two children and Sammy enjoyed the casual dinner in the garden. Teasing and lighthearted humor set the tone.

"Will you come again?" Tommy asked when Laurel and Mace got ready to leave. "And bring Sammy?"

"Of course."

Laurel drew in a soft breath and realized that she felt a measure of peace. The future, still uncertain, loomed before her, but she no longer felt alone. For the first time in her life, she had family. *Thank You, Lord. Thank You.*

After saying goodbye, Laurel and Mace stepped outside—and were met by a hailstorm of bullets. Recognizing the staccato of MP5s, Laurel dropped to the flagstone sidewalk, gathered Sammy to her and protected him with her own body. She and Mace drew their weapons and, from their prone positions, returned fire.

But the men weren't aiming at her. They were aiming at Mace, clearly wanting him out of the way. One man went so far as to get out of the car and head her way. He turned back when he saw Caleb, weapon at the ready, join them.

All three kept firing until the car had rounded a corner.

By that time, Shelley had joined them, a Glock

in her hands. "I put the children in the back room. What happened?"

Mace looked grim. "Someone just tried to take Laurel and kill me."

TWELVE

For the second time in four days, Mace and Laurel sat in the uncomfortable chairs of the detective's office and answered questions. For the second time, they parsed out answers with an eye to telling the truth but refraining from making assumptions. Trusting the police was an option they could not afford.

Shelley had had to come in for questioning, too, as the attack had happened at her house.

After the interrogation, she called Jake and arranged for the four of them to meet at S&J headquarters. In the rental truck, Mace steered expertly through the late-evening traffic.

When he pulled the car to a stop at S&J headquarters, he didn't immediately open the door. "I know it seems they have us on the run, but the game's not over. Not by a long shot."

Laurel warmed to the determination in his voice and the big hand he laid on her shoulder, but the guilt of having brought trouble to Shelley's family was almost more than she could bear.

In her office, Shelley ran to Laurel, threw her arms around her. "Remember, you're not alone. We're in this together."

"Thank you. You don't know how much I needed to hear that. But I'm sorry I brought this trouble to your door. I didn't think it through."

Shelley shook her head. "None of that."

Remorse swept through Laurel at the danger she'd put Shelley's family in. "If I leave, maybe the goons the Collective keeps sending after me will follow and let you live in peace. I was selfish in coming here."

Sensing her distress, Sammy pressed closer to her leg.

"There'll never be peace as long as groups like Winston's exist. They feed on hate and fear," Jake said. "You were right to come here. We're family."

His attitude toward her had done an about-face. Maybe he was coming to accept the possibility that they might be brother and sister. Or maybe he wanted to please Shelley, who so obviously wanted the connection to be real. From what Laurel knew about the brother and sister, Jake had always considered himself Shelley's protector, even now.

Laurel offered a tremulous smile. Shelley and Jake were both more generous than she deserved.

Shelley seemed to grow in stature as she paced the room, her energy a force to be reckoned with. For a moment, Laurel actually felt sorry for whoever was behind this. Shelley wouldn't rest until they were behind bars. For all her small size, she was as tenacious as a bulldog and didn't back down from a fight.

Laurel blinked back tears at Shelley and Jake's staunch support. The knowledge that she had family and friends who were willing to stand beside her was the most precious gift she'd ever received.

"I am so sorry," she said. "If something had happened to Chloe or Tommy…" Her voice choked.

"They're okay," Shelley said. "Caleb's with them. We've posted a couple of operatives outside the house. We'll rotate them until this is over."

"How did they find us?" Laurel asked. "We weren't followed. Mace did several SDRs on our way to your house." Surveillance detour routes were standard procedure for military and civilian operators.

Mace looked at her jacket. "A tracking device."

"There's no way someone could have planted anything there." Realization came with a start. "Except at the prison." She and Mace had had to check their belongings in a locker. Anyone with the code could have gotten to her jacket.

Painstakingly, she went through every inch of the jacket and found what she was looking for embedded in a seam. The device was state-of-the-art.

Mace took it and squashed it beneath his heel.

Laurel shuddered at what her carelessness had brought to her newfound family.

"If the Collective's been tracking us since our visit to the prison," Mace said, "then they know the location of the safe house."

"We'll find another one," Shelley promised and gripped Laurel's hand.

"That won't be necessary," Mace said. "I'll take her to my cabin."

Mace felt more than saw the surprised glances Shelley and Jake exchanged. It was well-known at S&J that he never invited people, even friends, to his cabin. Set deep within the Georgia woods, it was his haven, his refuge, his sanctuary.

The apartment in town was a convenience. The cabin was home.

Within ten minutes, he and Laurel were on their way, leaving the trappings of civilization behind with every mile.

What would Laurel think of the cabin? Would she be put off by the rustic atmosphere, the plain furnishings, the lack of neighbors?

Impatient with his thoughts, he pulled up to a mom-and-pop store not far from his place. After a quick shopping trip, he drove the last few miles to the cabin. There, he hefted the box of supplies he'd bought. Food, toilet paper and an extra-large bag of dog food.

Sammy jumped out of the truck, sniffed the ground and then ran around the cabin. When he returned, he gave a loud bark which Mace took as approval of the new digs.

Laurel had said little on the trip to the cabin.

He knew what was eating her. Guilt left nasty teeth marks, and right now they were all over her, chewing their way into her heart. He was dealing with his own guilt fest as well, unable to shake the suspicion that by asking Tony to gather information on the Collective, he'd effectively signed the man's death warrant.

There was a saying on the street: snitches get stitches. What had happened to Tony proved it.

She carried her bag into the cabin. "Where do you want me?"

He pointed down the hall. "Second room on the left. It's got its own bathroom."

With Sammy bringing up the rear, she walked down the hallway.

Mace heard the bedroom door shut. He'd give her time to deal with her feelings. Not too much time, though. It was one thing to accept guilt, another to wallow in it.

Though they'd had a meal at Shelley and Caleb's home, Mace knew that the last hours had taken a lot out of Laurel. With that in mind, he heated up a can of soup and made grilled cheese sandwiches.

He knocked on her door. "Soup's on."

"Not hungry."

He pushed open the door. "Too bad. You need to eat."

"You can't know what I need."

"Okay," he agreed easily. "But Sammy needs to eat."

Another wave of guilt chased across her face. "Of course. What was I thinking…?"

"You weren't thinking. You don't want to eat, then we work."

"Work?"

"You heard me. Work." He gave her shirt and slacks a disparaging look. "Change into something you can move in and meet me in the basement."

He'd intrigued her. He saw that. Better she be curious than steeped in guilt. "Like I said, we've got work to do. You have five minutes." He snapped his fingers. "C'mon, Sammy. You're hungry, aren't you?"

Sammy looked to Laurel. "Go on, boy," she said.

Mace hadn't liked coming down on her that

way, but he'd had to pull her out of the quagmire of guilt into which she'd fallen.

Guilt didn't solve anything. He ought to know.

THIRTEEN

Laurel looked around the basement that had been turned into a professionally equipped work-out room. Weights, cardio machines and every-thing in between had been carefully selected and placed. There was even a Jacuzzi to ease tired muscles at the end of a workout.

"This is really something," she said.

"It took a while to put together, but I knew what I wanted. I worked on it a bit at a time, in between jobs and when I could afford it. It suits me."

At one time, she'd owned the gym. She'd worked out alongside men who outweighed her by a hundred or more pounds and had held her own. Now, on the days when the pain had a stranglehold on her, she could barely lift her arm over her head.

"You don't have to pretend with me." His voice unexpectedly softened. "I know."

"Know what?"

"That you're in so much pain on some days that you can barely think straight. That even the smallest movement causes you to want to scream in agony. I know," he repeated. "I saw it the first time we met. The way you held your arm close, as though you couldn't bear to move it even an inch. What have you done for it?"

"You name it, I've tried it." She couldn't keep the bitterness from her voice as she thought of the brutal rehab she'd endured to restore full motion in her arm and shoulder.

Mace planted his hands on his hips. "Name it."

"Name what?"

"Your pain. Give it a name. Talk to it. Yell at it. Tell it that you're in charge, not it."

"Are you crazy?"

"Not so you'd notice." His grin was a flash of white teeth.

"You want me to name my pain and that's supposed to make it all go away." She nearly rolled her eyes at the ridiculousness of it.

"No. It won't go away. Not at first. Maybe never. But you can give it a name. Talk to it. Ask it why it's doing this to you."

"Look, Mace, you're a good guy, but—"

"I'm off my rocker," he finished the sentence for her.

"Something like that."

"Do you know how I met Jake?"

The change of subject took her by surprise. "Overseas, I guess. When you were both serving."

"Wrong. We met in rehab."

"Oh."

"Jake came home with a busted-up leg. He could barely walk. It still gives him fits at times, but he's worked through it for the most part."

"And you?"

"I came home with a busted-up body." His voice darkened, as did the look in his eyes.

What did that mean?

"I spent nine months in a prison camp. It was...rough."

Images too horrible to contemplate swirled through her mind. Terrorists bragged about how they broke American soldiers with their inhumane treatment. "Look, we don't have to talk about this. Not now."

"Don't worry. I'm not going to share all the details with you. Just know that I have some experience with pain." The wry twist of his lips underscored what must have been a massive understatement.

"I'm sorry." She winced at the total inadequacy of the words. She knew a sudden longing to reach out, to touch him, to wipe away the memories of what he'd endured.

"Don't be. I made it through. But I had to learn to deal with it. It was that or go crazy. So I named the pain. I yelled at it. I begged it to stop. Finally, I accepted it."

Intrigued despite herself, she leaned forward. "What did you call it?"

"Ralph."

"Ralph?"

"After my uncle Ralph. Great-uncle, to be precise. He was my mama's uncle. We used to go visit his place in Tennessee when my brother and I were kids. He had a cabin in the Great Smokies. It had running water, but that was about it."

"So why'd you name your pain after him?"

"Uncle Ralph could be a scary dude. He liked to take out his false teeth and clack them at us."

"You're making that up." The whole thing was too ridiculous to be true.

Mace put his hand to his brow and gave a smart salute. "Scout's honor. Uncle Ralph took out his teeth and made this clickety-clack noise at my brother and me. Scared my brother half to death. I was made of sterner stuff and actually touched them one time when Uncle Ralph took them out."

"What happened?"

"They near bit my finger off. Uncle Ralph laughed so hard that his toupee fell off."

"Okay. Now I know you're making it up."

"Well, maybe the part about the toupee."

"And the teeth?"

"The teeth were real."

They were straying from the subject, and she honestly wanted to know how he'd learned to live with the pain by giving it a name.

"Back to naming your pain. Did it help?"

"Not at first. It turns out that Ralph and I had this kind of love-hate relationship, heavy on the hate. But when I started talking to him…it… I learned I could control the pain. Giving it a name took away some of its power."

"You really talked to Ralph?"

"The pain. Not my uncle. He was long gone by then. I told Ralph that he was kicking my butt, and that I was tired of it. Then I told him it was my turn."

"Did he answer?" Despite her skepticism, she found that she really wanted to know.

"You could say that. He kicked my butt some more. Then he started backing off. Just a little, but enough that I could get through the exercises without breaking down and crying like a baby."

"Did you do that whole pain scale thing," she asked, "like they have you do in PT?"

"Yeah. When I got back to the States, I did my share of PT. Like I said, that's where Jake and I met. Turns out we'd both named our pain. It's not real common, but it's gaining in popularity among therapists." Mace sent her a quizzical look. "What about it? Ready to give your pain a name?"

She didn't have to think about it. "Bob."

"Bob? Someone in particular or you just don't like the name?"

"Drill sergeant. He made my life miserable for six straight weeks. Yelled at me so loud that I was sure my eardrums were going to burst. Seems only fitting that I should give him some of his own back and yell at him."

Though all the sergeants had made life a misery for recruits, most had done so with the intent of turning them into soldiers. Robert "Bob" Chastain had had a different agenda: he'd liked inflicting as much punishment on the young men and women unfortunate enough to be assigned to his special brand of training.

He'd derived pleasure from humiliating them in front of the other recruits. He'd taken extra pleasure in singling out the two lone females, Laurel and Sarah. Whatever he required of the male recruits, he doubled—even quadrupled—for the females. In the end, Sarah hadn't been able to take it and had been discharged from the Army.

Mace drew her back to the present. "I'm guessing you do some kind of rotator cuff exercises."

She made a face. "You guessed right." She looked down at her right arm, folded protectively against her chest. "When things get bad, I know it's because I haven't exercised it enough. Trouble is, doing the therapy feels like I'm putting my shoulder through a shredder."

"Got it. We'll take it easy."

"We? You're not a therapist."

"I've been through enough therapy that I have everything but the shingle to hang on my door."

"I'm not sure." She avoided his gaze. "Having a colleague hear me cry like a baby isn't exactly high on my bucket list." She'd humiliated herself enough at PT by breaking down in tears when the pain had grown unbearable.

"You don't think I've done my share of the bawling-like-a-baby thing?"

She considered the supremely fit man who looked like he'd never shed a tear in his life. "It's hard to picture," she said at last.

"I know what it is to hurt so bad that you don't think you can take another breath." He reached for her hand, squeezed gently. "I'll help you. If it gets too much, you can quit."

"I'm not a quitter," she said, each syllable ground through her teeth like she was chewing cut glass.

"I didn't think you were. Drop your arm. Let it hang loose."

She did as he instructed. Immediately a hiss of pain buzzed through the air. She bit down on her tongue in a futile effort to control the wave of agony that rolled through her.

"Okay," Mace said. "Let's see what you've got. Raise your arm above your head and then reach as far as you can. Pretend you're reaching for the stars."

Laurel did as he instructed. Misery screamed through her shoulder. Only the knowledge that Mace was there to witness it enabled her to suck it up and keep stretching.

She wasn't certain how she felt that Mace had zeroed in on her pain. Part of her was annoyed that she'd failed to hide the agony that her shoulder and arm caused. She didn't like that he'd read her so easily. Another part was touched by his concern.

"Enough," he said when she could no longer hold back a groan.

She nearly wept with relief.

Mace kept his comments to a minimum. He felt every shaft of pain Laurel endured as though it were his own as she struggled to complete the exercises. She was a proud woman who would refuse sympathy just as he had refused the overtures on the part of his buddies who'd witnessed his struggles.

Understanding didn't mean it was easy for him to watch her push herself to a point past exhaustion. If he could have, he'd have taken the pain from her, but that wasn't possible, and so he clenched his jaw with every whimper she gave.

You can do it. The words never made it to his lips. Instead, he kept them locked inside, willing her to find the strength she needed. Surviving recovery was as much mental as physical.

When she completed the final set, she turned to him with a smile that was more a grimace. "Done. Three sets, as instructed."

"Congratulations."

Her shoulders drooped. "Thanks. I wish I felt like I was making progress."

"You are. You just can't see it."

She slumped onto a bench, braced her hands on her knees and let her head droop.

He offered a hand to help her up. Awareness thrummed between them at the casual contact. Without making more of the gesture than it warranted, he removed his hand, stuffed it in his pocket.

Laurel, too, had looked shaken at the touch. "After I get my breath back, I'll start again."

"You don't have—"

She gave him a look that told him to back off. He did.

When he judged her ready to start again, he hitched his chin at the equipment. Compassion warred with respect as he watched her push herself beyond her limits.

She did a set.

Beads of sweat popped out on her forehead, above her lip, down her shirt.

"Yell," Mace ordered. "Tell Bob to back off. Tell him he's not wanted here."

Laurel yelled. And yelled some more.

By the time she'd finished, she'd managed another set.

Mace gave her a thumbs-up. "What's your pain number, between one and ten?"

"Twenty-eight."

"Come on, soldier. Tell me the real number."

"Eight." She said it with a grudging tone. "Maybe seven and a half."

"Not bad. How's that compare to other days?"

"Better." The admission cost her. He saw it in the tightening of her lips. "Naming the pain...it might have helped." She flushed.

He quirked a brow. "Might have?"

"Might have."

"You'll be hurting soon."

"What's this *will be* stuff?"

"Okay. You're hurting. Take a breather. Then we do it again. Of course, if you'd prefer to quit..." He shrugged as though it made no difference to him either way.

"You don't play fair."

"No, I don't. But then neither does Bob."

Mace put Laurel through her paces. Every time she flinched, every time she hissed out a pain-filled breath, he wanted to stop, to tell her they'd done enough, but the determination in her face, the fire in her eyes, told him she needed this. More, wanted it.

The lady was forged in steel. He knew too

well the pain he was putting her through, knew she had to be screaming at him inside her head, but she didn't say anything, other than to yell at Bob at the top of her lungs.

When he judged she'd done as much as she could, probably more than she should, he called a halt. "Enough."

Laurel sank to the floor. If he hadn't been there, she'd have probably been in tears at the end of the session. As it was, she only breathed deeply, her exhales coming in labored pants.

"What's the number now?" he asked.

She appeared to think about it. "Nine. It went up." The querulous tone had him smiling.

"That's good. It means you worked through it and kept on going. Maybe you should thank Bob."

"Thank him?"

"Tell him that he did a good job of letting you know when you'd had enough."

"Enough was thirty minutes ago." She made a face at him.

Ordinarily, he would have grinned, but not this time. He was too aware of her and how she made him feel. "It also lets you know that you're still alive. Still kicking."

"Is that what Ralph did for you?"

Mace didn't need to think about it. "Ralph was there when I needed him."

"And sometimes when you didn't?"

He inclined his head. "And sometimes when I didn't."

"You really think I should thank Bob?"

"It's up to you. If you're not ready for that, don't sweat it. Maybe another time. In the meantime, you're holding your arm easier."

She looked down at her arm, a surprised expression moving over her features. "I guess I am."

"What does that tell you?"

"I don't know."

He gave a faint smile at the reluctance in her eyes. "You don't want to admit that the pain is less. I get it. I didn't want to admit it either the first time I gave my pain a name and yelled at it."

"You didn't?"

He thought he detected hope in her voice. He understood the being-afraid-to-believe-it-might-help hope. As they said, been there, done that.

"Nope. I didn't. But I couldn't deny that the pain was less. Just a bit. It still hurt like a bear had been chewing on me and then spit me out, but I was handling it better."

Laurel hung her head. "You're right—I don't want to admit it. Because it sounds too weird to be true. But my arm isn't screaming with pain right now like it normally would be after a workout."

"I'd call that progress."

"Yeah. Progress." She looked up. "Thanks. I owe you."

"Don't thank me. Thank Bob." He gave her a straight look. "And you don't owe me a thing."

FOURTEEN

Laurel wasn't ready to thank Bob. Yet. A practical woman, she needed more evidence upon which to base a conclusion than one experience, but she couldn't deny that she was looser, more in tune with herself. Salt from rivulets of sweat rimmed her skin, but it felt good, as though she were sweating the pain out of her.

A tender mercy from the Lord. She had no doubt that He had placed Mace at the right time at the right place to help her. Despite Mace's claim that he wasn't a believer, she'd felt his concern. That kind of compassion was rooted in the Lord.

Even as exhaustion burned through her shoulders, arms and neck, she said a silent prayer of thanksgiving. *Lord, thank You for bringing Mace into my life.*

"There are shadows in your eyes. I thought you'd have sweated them out by now." A teasing light sparked in his eyes.

She smiled as she knew he'd intended, then her smile vanished. "I'm still thinking about what might have happened at Shelley and Caleb's house. The children…" Tears clogged her throat, while the lethal blades of guilt sliced away at her heart.

"You're doing it again."

"What?"

"Taking on guilt that isn't yours. You're too smart for that. Blaming yourself for what happened is stupid. And I know you're not stupid." She must have looked unconvinced, for he added, "This is not on you. None of it. Lean on me. For a minute, if that's all you can allow yourself. You don't have to carry everything all by yourself."

There was such gentleness in his voice, such care. When was the last time she had allowed herself to lean on anyone? For anything?

"I don't know how." With a start, she realized she'd spoken the words aloud.

"You're dead tired. It's a wonder you're still on your feet."

"I couldn't have slept. You knew that. That's why you hammered at me."

"Smart girl. Smart enough to know not to push yourself when you need rest. You could have called it quits after one set. Why did you keep going?"

"Probably for the same reason you do."

"I think it's more. You have to prove yourself. You always have to be the best. You're an overachiever. Best in your class at school. Best on any team you played on. Best in your Ranger training."

How had he known? "I've always had to prove myself," she said slowly. "To the mother who didn't want me. To the Army. To the Rangers. You're right that I always had to be the best. But not for the reasons you think."

"Why don't you tell me?"

She appeared to weigh that. "Does it matter?"

"I think so."

"You know about my mother." Her voice didn't break, and, for that, she was grateful. "I think I was about five when I discovered that Bernice didn't like being a mother. Kids, even little kids, know. But I kept trying.

"I always wondered why I wasn't enough. Why she couldn't love me. I worked extra hard, kept the trailer where we were living at the time spotless, made straight As, but nothing I did mattered.

"When I was twelve, she left me alone for six days. I had to go through the garbage at school, looking for scraps like an animal." The memory of hunger so sharp, so clawing, that it felt like she'd been stabbed multiple times crossed the years. "A teacher saw me, called child services."

"Let me guess. Foster care."

"Yeah. But it was good. The people who took me in wanted children and could never have them. The mom, Stella, was everything Bernice wasn't." Now emotion roughened her voice, but she kept going. "She was there for my school play. She was there when I made the seventh-grade honor roll. She was...there.

"After Bernice returned, I wanted to stay there with Stella and Bruce, but CPS sent me back, said a child's place was with her mother, no matter that the so-called mother was nothing of the sort. The social worker read her the riot act, then gave her a slap on the wrist, but that was it." Laurel kept the tears at bay, barely, recalling Stella crying when the lady from Child Protective Services arrived.

"I'm sorry."

"Don't be. It made me what I am. I'm not Bernice. I'm not a victim." It seemed important that she make this clear.

"Never said you were."

"But you were feeling sorry for me. Don't. I'm who I made myself, along with the Lord's help. He has never forsaken me."

"You don't have to prove yourself to me."

"The man I told you about, who died in my arms?" At his nod, she continued, "That soldier—scarcely more than a boy—died saving my life. He sacrificed his life for mine. I can never forget that, never repay what he did."

"Don't go down that road. There's nothing there."

Remembered pain worked its way through her heart.

"You have to know that it wasn't your fault. You don't do yourself any favors by taking on what isn't yours. Just like today."

"You make it sound simple."

"Not at all. Nothing about it is simple. You can choose to move on or to bury yourself in guilt."

"You're doing it again—simplifying what isn't simple."

"I'm just trying to make you see that you have to make a choice."

"I've wanted to be a Ranger since one came to speak at career day at school. He was everything I'd dreamed of becoming—strong, courageous, committed. He made the work sound important and I knew I wanted to be a part of that."

"You made it."

"I made it, but I don't know if I can keep it."

Snap out of it. The stern words, uttered only in her mind, caused Laurel to straighten her spine. What was she doing, confiding in Mace that way? She'd never shared those feelings with anyone about the soldier who died, not even the Army shrink assigned to her.

She was a job to Mace. Nothing more. She'd

do well to remember that. With that pep talk, she told herself she was in control of the situation, but when she looked up to find his gaze warm upon her, she knew she'd only been fooling herself. Though she'd known other soldiers, Mace stood out. The honor which defined him served as a beacon to those who needed help.

"Who are you, aside from being a Ranger?" His quietly asked question erased any feeling of control she'd fooled herself into believing she possessed.

"I don't know." That was honest, she reflected. Honest and terrifying. If she wasn't a Ranger, what was she?

"Like I said, you're smart. You'll figure it out."

"I'm afraid you give me too much credit." The death of the young soldier had caused her to question everything she'd believed in. After this mission—and that was how she saw it, a mission—she had to make a decision. If she couldn't return to being a Ranger, she still had to live her life.

She couldn't afford to do nothing. Nor did the idea have any appeal.

She knew her confusion was evident on her face. She wanted to blank her expression, to keep her uncertainty and doubts to herself. Mace saw far too much. His perception was one of the things she liked best about him, but it had its downside, such as now, when he read her so clearly.

"Enough about me." She hoped he'd take the hint and switch subjects.

"When you're ready," he said, "I'm here."

The matter-of-fact offer was as unexpected as it was sweet. She didn't know if she'd ever be ready to share more about herself. Some memories cut too deep. If she opened them up and exposed them to the light of day, they might bleed until there was nothing left.

She'd expected her feelings for him would have faded, not grown, but they were stronger than ever, her emotions in a tailspin. He wasn't the most attractive man she'd ever met, though he came close.

His appeal went far deeper than mere physical looks, deep enough that a woman could lose herself in him.

Laurel pulled out of her spiraling thoughts. A relationship was far down on her list of priorities. Making Ranger had dominated her thinking for as long as she could remember. Every decision was weighed against that goal.

But Mace Ransom had changed things. He was annoying, bossy and far too fond of getting his own way. On the other hand, he was a skilled operative who brought daring and courage to the job and had saved her life more than once.

And he had a way of listening that made her

want to open up about things she'd never before shared. Some of the loneliness that she carried with her receded when she was with him. He tempted her to take down the barriers she'd spent a lifetime erecting.

Almost.

"Let's get something in your stomach," Mace said. After cleaning up, they met in the kitchen. He looked at the congealed soup and hardened sandwiches he'd prepared earlier and tossed them. In their place, he fixed scrambled eggs, bacon and toast. Comfort food.

They ate companionably. When they had finished, he stacked the dishes in the dishwasher, wiped the table and sat opposite Laurel.

Sammy settled at her feet.

"We talked about me. Tell me about you," she said.

To his surprise, Mace found he wanted to confide in Laurel, to tell her of the past that shadowed him to this day. Still, he hesitated. Did he really want to tell her—tell anyone—of the shame he carried with him every day?

He started with the present and spoke about Tony's murder. "I promised him money if he came through for me with information about the Collective. He must have gotten too close, because they killed him."

"You can't know that."

"No, I can't. But it's a fair guess."

Silence hung in the room before Laurel said, "Someone told me not too long ago to not take on what isn't mine. Whoever killed Tony is responsible for his death. Not you."

"Thank you for that, but there's more."

He started talking, the words increasing in speed as the memories gathered within him and spilled over. Soon, he couldn't stop the flow of words and allowed them free rein.

"Our unit was sent on a recon mission. We were ambushed and holed up in an abandoned house, more of a hut, really, for three-and-a-half days."

Laurel's swift intake of breath confirmed that she understood the significance of the time involved.

Most soldiers knew that seventy-two hours was stretching the limit for endurance. Add to that limited food and water and only a few hours' sleep, and you had the makings of an escalating crisis. Spec Ops teams like Rangers, Delta Force and SEALs could stretch that seventy-two into a few more hours, but not by much.

Mace's team was already down two men. Those remaining had taken turns keeping watch and returning enemy fire, but they were reaching the end of even their elite training.

"More than thirty enemy troops surrounded us," he continued. "I was one of six men left.

We had intel that we had to get to the unit commander. We knew we weren't going to survive. Not all of us. So we drew straws." He took a steadying breath as he relived that time.

"I got the short straw. That meant I had to leave my buddies behind and get the information out. They held off the enemy long enough for me to make my escape." Pain chased through him at the dark memory.

"Leaving them—knowing they were going to die so that I could get through to our people—tore me apart. I wanted to refuse and knew that I couldn't. Any one of us would have felt the same. It would have been far easier to stay with my unit and go down fighting than leave my brothers behind." Guilt roughened his voice, and he swallowed noisily to rid himself of the lump that had lodged in his throat. "That's what we were to each other. Brothers."

"You did what you had to."

"Did I? I don't know. I got the intel to our people. It was actionable, and I was called a hero." He gave a harsh laugh as the echo of memories stabbed at his heart with poisonous tips. "Do you believe that? A hero. I got a medal and a pat on the back. All I had to do was to abandon my friends. They were the real heroes. I never wore the medal, never wanted to. It's still in its box. I don't know why I kept it."

Phrases like *sole survivor* **and** *hero* **had been**

tossed about. He didn't wear either label well. Especially when they weren't true.

"A few months later, I was captured. I had time to think on what had happened. I wondered if subconsciously I let myself be taken because I'd left my friends behind to die. When I was in that cesspool of a prison camp, I was certain that everyone had abandoned me. Including God."

Twin lines of concern worked their way across her brow. "You're wrong. You know that, don't you? You're about as wrong as a man can be."

"What do you know about it?"

"I know that the Lord has a plan for you and you wallowing in a mire of self-pity and guilt isn't it. The Lord will carry your burdens but not your baggage." Her tone gentled. "He doesn't expect perfection from us, only a desire to try to do better. That's what keeps me going. Sometimes it's the only thing that keeps me going."

Her absolute certainty of the Lord's wisdom shook him. At the same time, he resented it. And her. "I get where you're going with this, but you'll have to excuse me if I can't handle your Pollyanna beliefs."

Regret filled him immediately that he'd spoken so harshly to her. "I'm sorry. I had no right to speak to you that way."

"No problem."

But it was. Hurt glazed her eyes.

Could she be right about the Lord having a

plan for him? What was there about this woman that had him thinking things that were totally unlike him? With an effort, he shored up his resolve. He and the Lord had parted ways years ago. He'd abandoned God around the same time that God had abandoned him. Funny how that worked.

"The Lord is always at our side," she said softly. "He never leaves us. If there's any leaving to be done, it's on our part. It's up to us to find our way back to Him."

"If you say so."

"I don't say so. He does. The Lord is all-powerful. When we draw on that power, we know we're on the right path."

Anger surged inside him. What did she know about it? Memories too painful to face were his constant companion, his albatross, his cross. There would be no absolution for him. Not now. Not ever.

Now that he'd taken them out and shone the light of day upon them, he felt worse than ever. He'd been right to hide them in a faraway corner of his mind, where nothing could reach them.

To his relief, she didn't try to talk him out of it. Laurel only waited, and the feelings within him spilled forth. "I'm broken inside," he said, more to himself than to her, "and probably always will be."

"Tell me the rest of it, what you didn't tell me earlier, about your time in the prison camp."

Grateful that she'd left the subject of the Lord and His forgiveness, Mace answered readily enough. "After I was captured, I was put in a hole. Once a day, food was thrown down, along with a bottle of water. There was no toilet, not even a bucket. I didn't see the sun for months. What the guards did to the prisoners... Finally, I was traded for another prisoner of war, but I wasn't the same." He shook his head, as though the gesture could wipe away the horrors.

"No one is."

The words grated against the memory of those awful months, and something raw boiled over inside of him. He was held in a hole in the ground and went for months without seeing the sun. The only bit of light he caught was daylight lining the edges of the wooden top of the earthen hole. "That's pretty glib for someone who's never been a POW."

"You're right."

He searched her gaze for any sign of deceit and saw only unvarnished honesty. Laurel hadn't been a prisoner of war, but she'd suffered her own share of pain. He'd seen the agony she suffered as she struggled to get through the exercises.

The contrition in her voice shamed him. She'd only been trying to help, and he'd bitten her head off. "I don't talk about that time much." Make that none at all. And he didn't know why he was doing so now. Once this was over, he and Laurel would go their separate ways.

That was the way it was. That was the way he wanted it.

Laurel absorbed the words but remained silent long enough that the shadows in the room shifted. What could she say to this man who had endured so much, including the loss of his faith?

They needed a break. "It's past time that I took Sammy out," she said.

"Good idea. We can walk the perimeter."

Sammy barked his joy at going out. He would never prance impatiently as did some dogs at the idea of a walk, but she felt his pleasure.

Together, the three of them walked the property line. She was surprised at the extent of Mace's property.

"It's beautiful here," she said.

"I like it. I needed a place like this, even if I can't make it here as much as I'd like."

She felt much of the tension drain from her in this slice of beauty.

A rabbit darted in front of them. Sammy gave no notice, too well-trained to give chase.

Mace had shared an important part of his past with her. She wanted to reach out, to smooth her hands over his jaw, to wipe away the tension that held it with such rigid pain. Her gaze dropped to his hands and she noted again the deliberate, controlled action with which he used them. Not a wasted motion.

A scar on his hand snagged her attention, a jagged line tracing from his knuckles to his wrist.

"A glass bottle and I got up close and personal," he said in answer to her unspoken question. "My unit and I were assigned to protect a school. We thought the threat was only from the outside, but one of the teachers was a plant by a terrorist group. When it became clear that we were going to beat back the insurgents, the teacher showed her true colors. She went after the girls, but I got in the way."

Of course he had. Mace would never allow an innocent to be hurt if he could stop it, even at a cost to himself.

Educating girls was considered a sin among many Middle Eastern sects. It wasn't unheard of for a zealot to embed herself into a school for the express purpose of destroying it. Laurel shook her head at the waste.

"The girls…did they survive?"

"We got them to a refugee camp that took them in. What those girls suffered—" he shook his head "—just to get a bit of education, made me want to knock some sense into kids here who don't realize what they have."

The hands that had moved with such assurance now rubbed agitatedly together. As though aware of the telltale gesture, he slammed a fist into his palm and left it there.

He looked vulnerable. How could that be? Strong. Determined. Courageous. Those were words she associated with Mace. But vulnerable? No. From the moment she and Mace had met, she'd admired his confidence, his boldness, his conviction. But beneath all that, there lay scars. Scars that ran deep.

Once again, she experienced the urge to smooth her hand over his jaw. Once again, she resisted.

"They got to you, didn't they?" she asked. "Those girls. It was the same with me the first time I stepped inside a school outside of Jalal-Abad. All those eager young faces, so excited to learn, to find out what was beyond their village. I went back to our camp and found every book and magazine I could and delivered them.

"I'll never forget the look on the girls' faces. It was like a thousand Christmases and birthdays rolled into one. Some of those girls had never seen a book outside the school, much less had one of their own. They touched the books with a kind of reverence I'd never seen before."

Her remembered joy in the moment died as other memories took its place.

She'd witnessed firsthand the courage of the

Afghani people who fought their enemies, even knowing they couldn't win. Those same people had assisted American soldiers, risking and sometimes giving their own lives to put an end to the carnage taking place in their country.

Her men had done their best to provide a speck of pleasure for the children, sharing little gifts from home, like candy and magazines. She had had nothing from home to share but had bought treats for children who had so very little. Few had shoes but never complained about hot, blistered feet or empty bellies.

And then the explosion had happened, claiming her comrades' lives as well as injuring her and Sammy.

The grueling days and weeks of therapy that followed had tested her in ways she'd never thought to be tested. The pain had been excruciating, and at times she wasn't certain she'd make it to the other end, but she hadn't given up.

She'd told herself it didn't matter that she'd had no one to visit her, no one to cry with her, no one to encourage her as did the other patients. She'd told herself that it didn't matter that she never received letters or care packages. She told herself she didn't need anyone. She'd told herself lie after lie after lie. Until the lies didn't make her feel any better, and she wanted to scream under the weight of them.

Only then did she start to tell herself the truth and start to improve.

It was over. Time to move on. And still the acuteness of her aloneness lingered. Sammy had kept her sane. Knowing that he depended on her had given her the incentive to keep going when she might otherwise have given up.

"Why are you asking me all of this?" she asked.

"Maybe for the same reason you asked about my past."

She cocked her head. "So what have you learned?"

"That you don't run from a problem or duck it. That you march straight through it until you come out the other end."

"You got all that from what I told you?"

"I got all that from what you didn't tell me." His gaze met hers, a challenge. "What did you learn about me?"

"You're a straight shooter. You don't waver. You do what you have to despite the cost to yourself."

"You're way off the mark. You think I don't sometimes want to chuck it all and take the easy way?"

She couldn't picture Mace ever taking the easy way with anything. He was steel through and through. Making Ranger took grit, guts and a whole lot of heart. She ought to know.

"What about you? You ever want to take the easy way out?"

"When Bernice died, I thought of not going to the service. I actually considered not attending my own mother's funeral." The memory lashed her soul with stinging stripes.

She lifted her gaze. "When you're looking for answers, the only way to look is up."

"You're pretty amazing."

"I'm not amazing at all. But I keep trying. Each day I try to be better than I was the day before. That's what the Lord asks of me, so that's what I ask of myself." The look she shot him was full of challenge. "What do you think the Lord asks of you?"

The question startled him. "I don't know."

"Maybe you should find out."

"Maybe I should."

FIFTEEN

"What do you know about Winston's wife?" Laurel asked over a breakfast of eggs, bacon and hash browns two mornings later. They'd spent the previous day chasing down leads that had gone nowhere. Discouragement had sat heavily on her shoulders at the wasted day.

Nothing had been said about their conversation of two nights ago. Probably best that way. She didn't need further complications in her life, and Mace Ransom was definitely a complication. A very handsome, very intriguing complication, but a complication all the same. It was best for him and for her to keep things on a professional level.

"Not much. She stood by him during the trial, then disappeared from public life. Word is that she stayed at the same house, her family home. She refused to give interviews at the time of the trial. After Ronnie was sentenced, she continued to refuse. The press moved on to another story."

"Maybe we can learn something from her. Ronnie may have let something slip around her and likely doesn't think she's smart enough to do anything with it. Men like that always see women as inferior."

Mace nodded thoughtfully. "You ever think of going into profiling? You only just met him and you already know what makes him tick."

"I've known men like him all my life. Bernice…" She paused, swallowed. "Bernice attracted that kind of man. They're bullies, the lot of them. They have to put others down, either physically or emotionally, to feel that they have any worth. Anyway, it might be helpful to pay Mrs. Winston a visit. And I'm not convinced she isn't involved somehow."

Mace aimed a small salute in Laurel's direction. "I like the way you think. I'll get her address and then we can drop in on her."

"Unannounced?"

"No sense in giving her time to prepare herself or notify Winston's associates."

"I like the way you think." A framed quote on a shelf snared her interest. "May I?" she asked, gesturing to it.

At Mace's nod, Laurel picked up the finely worked piece of calligraphy and read it to herself. *The world breaks everyone; afterward many are strong at the broken places.* She recognized the quote from Hemingway's *A Farewell to Arms*.

She thought of Mace and what he'd shared with her. His strength and honor would always define him, as would his courage and integrity. "It's perfect." Unspoken were the words *You're pretty perfect, too*.

So much for keeping her feelings on the professional level she'd touted to herself only moments ago.

Mace came to stand next to her and, unexpectedly, skimmed his hand across her jaw. A shiver skittered down her spine, and she forgot her resolve of only minutes ago.

Laurel turned and drew closer to him. At the same time, an arc of awareness sparked between them.

She saw her surprise reflected in the dark irises of his eyes. Was he as taken aback as she at what had just happened? She hoped so. She didn't want to be in this—whatever it was—by herself. So close were they that she could see the bristle of whiskers, hear the slow intake of his breath, feel the beat of his heart.

This moment would forever be engraved on her mind, in her heart.

She found his hand, and, with infinite slowness, brought it to her lips. His intake of breath and the faint trembling of his fingers were telling.

"I have feelings for you, Laurel. You have to know that."

His words wended themselves around her heart.

"I can't promise anything," he said, his voice low but nonetheless compelling for it. "Not as long as the Collective is active. Not as long as you're a target. Keeping you safe has to be my priority."

She didn't challenge him with the assertion that she could keep herself safe as she might once have. Where was he going with this? And did she want to go there with him?

As much as she admired Mace, she didn't know if she could accept his lack of belief. Her faith was integral to her sense of self. And then there was her promise to herself to never become involved with a soldier again.

Two nights ago, she'd convinced herself that what she felt for him had been the result of the danger and intensity of the day's events. She'd been exhausted, ready to drop in her tracks.

This morning, she'd told herself that she didn't need the complication of a relationship, especially a relationship with someone as appealing as Mace Ransom, in her life. Now she wasn't so certain.

Something had changed between them. Something important, so important that she couldn't

put a name to it even if she wanted to…and she
wasn't at all sure that she did.

The sun beat down on the asphalt road on the
way to Jenni-Grace Winston's home and blistered the sky with streaks of white.

Mace shielded his eyes and squinted. He'd
grown accustomed to the heat of Afghanistan,
the dry, searing burn of it. Back in the States for
a couple of years now, he was still struggling to
adjust to the energy-sapping humidity of a Georgia summer.

He glanced at Laurel, quiet and composed.
They'd left Sammy at the cabin, much to the
German shepherd's displeasure. He considered
himself Laurel's protector, but a visit to the Win-
stons' home with him in tow hadn't seemed a
good idea.

Mace smiled, thinking of the big dog who was
still serving his country, though in a different
manner than that for which he'd been trained.
Sammy was a true American hero, far more so
than Mace would ever be.

His thoughts turned to Laurel's challenge to
him, to discover what the Lord wanted of him. It
humbled him in ways he could never have imagined. What could the Lord want of someone as
flawed as him?

The absolute certainty in her voice when she
spoke of the Lord had both irritated and riveted

him. He didn't doubt that she believed every word she'd said, that God would forgive him of his sins and turn them into virtues. How could that be, he wondered, acutely aware of how deep those sins ran.

There were times when he could almost bring himself to believe again. It was the sensation he experienced whenever he thought about Laurel. Which was most of the time.

Her faith shone in everything she did, everything she said, everything she was. When he had kissed her outside the prison and again in the truck with the pigs, he'd felt as though a chink had broken through the wall of disbelief he had erected years ago, as if he could absorb her faith and goodness through the small contact.

Somehow, Laurel and belief in the Lord had mixed together, until he couldn't separate the two.

He was moving too fast. Or, more precisely, his feelings for her were moving too fast. It had been the same with the teacher who'd turned out to be a CIA operative. She had betrayed him in the worst way possible and eroded his ability to trust.

He knew that Laurel would never deceive him in that way, but his heart was still bruised by the battering it had taken.

"What did your research tell you about the mysterious Mrs. Winston?" Mace asked in an attempt to take his thoughts off both Laurel and the Lord. Ever since their decision to call on Jenni-Grace Winston, Laurel had been reading up on the lady.

"I'm trying to understand what kind of woman would marry a man like Ronnie Winston."

"Don't keep me in suspense. Tell me."

Laurel grimaced. "I ended up with more questions than answers. She comes from money. Old money."

Mace understood the distinction. Old money was superior to new money. Though times were changing, many people clung to such outdated beliefs.

"She was a debutante at eighteen, attended Ole Miss University and graduated with honors in business management.

"Her father bred horses," Laurel continued. "When he and her mother died in a boating accident when she was only twenty, they left her a tidy inheritance. Not a fortune, but enough that she could live comfortably—very comfortably— for the rest of her life. Until the trial, she'd been active in civic and social affairs and served on the boards of several charities. So why marry Winston?"

"What did you come up with?"

"That's what we're going to find out."

Jenni-Grace Winston was beautifully dressed and groomed, as only a true Southern lady could be, in a silk sweater set paired with a couture-cut skirt, a single strand of pearls around her slender neck. With her genteel manners and in her designer clothes, she and Ronnie presented a study in contrasts.

Content to watch the lady, Laurel let Mace make the introductions. She took in the surroundings, the marble foyer with its crystal chandelier and portraits of dour-faced ancestors, and the graciously appointed parlor, the hallmark of a Southern home. The faded pastel upholstery and hand-rubbed rosewood spoke of taste far more than could any coldly modern furnishings.

To her mind, Shelley and Caleb's cheerfully cluttered bungalow with flowers spilling from fat pots was far more appealing.

Jenni-Grace was as far removed from Ronnie as a designer suit was from a Goodwill castoff. So why had she married a man so obviously beneath her on the social ladder?

Love made people go against the grain at times, but this pairing verged on the ludicrous. Why, Laurel asked herself again. What had Jenni-Grace Winston seen in the crude and roughly spoken Ronnie?

Money? Perhaps. Certainly, Winston had made a great deal of money from the Collective's various enterprises before he was sent to prison, but Jenni-Grace had her own fortune. The allure of a "bad boy"? Laurel suppressed a shudder as she recalled Winston's vulgar words and manner. That couldn't be enough.

"Mrs. Winston," Mace began, "we're here to learn anything we can about how your husband is managing to run the Collective from prison."

Laurel approved of his straightforward manner. Though Jenni-Grace might love Ronnie, that didn't mean she was blind to his doings. How could she be when his crimes had been plastered over the media for the months before and after his trial?

Jenni-Grace fluttered manicured hands. "I'm sure I don't know what you're talking about."

"You had to be aware of the crimes your husband was convicted of," Laurel said, speaking for the first time. "It makes sense you might know how he's getting his orders out."

"I won't sit here and have you say these awful things about my Ronnie." Jenni-Grace's voice quivered. Her hands moved to her pearls, and a tiny line of consternation formed a V between her perfectly groomed brows. "It wouldn't be the first time that corrupt lawyers and judges have put an innocent man in prison. How dare you come here—without invitation, I might add—and insult my husband and me?"

As she grew more agitated, she twisted the pearls back and forth, revealing a bit of green at the clasp, a figure of some sort.

Laurel had the sensation that she'd seen the figure before and tried to determine when it was.

As though aware of Laurel's scrutiny, Jenni-Grace righted the strand of pearls. "My husband has done nothing wrong. I'm content to wait for Ronnie to be vindicated and released."

Pity bubbled up inside of Laurel at the wife's blind faith and loyalty in a man who deserved neither.

"Your loyalty is admirable, Mrs. Winston," Mace said, "but surely you must see that it's misplaced." His lips had pulled tight, his easy expression vanished. Laurel shared the feeling. Mace was as frustrated as she was with Jenni-Grace and her blind devotion to a man who didn't deserve it.

"I see nothing of the kind." Jenni-Grace stood. "And I stand by my husband." Though Laurel and Mace each topped her by several inches, the woman managed to appear to be looking down her nose at them. "I'll thank you not to visit again. I'm sure you can see yourselves out."

Once they were in the car, Laurel turned to Mace. "She is either incredibly naive or she just doesn't care that her husband is a murderer."

"It would seem so."

"You don't think so?"

"I don't know what to think. The lady isn't stupid."

"Not stupid. But unaware, perhaps." But Laurel hadn't gotten that sense from Jenni-Grace Winston. On the contrary, except for the instance of twisting her pearl necklace, the lady had appeared cool and completely in control of herself. There was keen intelligence beneath the polished exterior.

A buzz from Mace's phone interrupted whatever he'd been about to say next, and he answered the call. "We'll be there in thirty," he said before hanging up. "That was Shelley. Rachel has translated part of the ledger. Shelley said we need to take a look at it."

On the way, they stopped to pick up Sammy, who greeted them with an enthusiastic bark. After feeding the shepherd and taking him for a short walk, Laurel and Sammy returned to the truck.

Excitement bubbled within her at the thought of actually reading the ledger. The ledger that had caused too many deaths, including that of Bernice. The ledger that had sent thugs after Laurel and Mace. The ledger that could put an end to the Collective once and for all.

"Let's do this," she said.

"Tell them what you found," Shelley said to Rachel.

The former FBI agent looked from Laurel and Mace to Shelley and Jake. "It took some doing to decipher the code." She darted a curious glance

Laurel's way. "The person who wrote this was too smart to put the information in a single binary code. She combined it with two others. In short, I had to excavate through three layers of encryption to decipher it."

Mace shifted in his chair.

"We don't doubt your skill," Shelley said gently. "Tell us what you found."

"Maybe you should see for yourself." Rachel tapped a few keys and pulled up a file from her laptop. "You may recognize some names."

Mace leaned in, then gave a low whistle. The encryption specialist was a master of the art of understatement. Three judges. Four city councilmen. A police chief. Police personnel from precincts all over the city.

"From the way the names are arranged into sections," Rachel said, "I think that each group pertains to a specific city. This one is probably Atlanta since I recognize a couple of the people listed. There are similar groupings throughout the book. Other cities. Other states. It'll go faster now that I have the code. It's just a matter of applying it to every listing and coming up with names."

"How many groupings are there?" Jake asked.

"Thirty-five."

The intake of breath by Shelley, Jake, Laurel and Mace told its own story.

"I knew the Collective had its hands everywhere," Laurel said, "but this goes way beyond what I dreamed."

"It's no dream," Jake said. "More like a nightmare."

"How do we fight this?" Laurel asked in a stunned whisper.

Mace had thought he'd understood the breadth of what they were dealing with in their mission to put an end to the Collective, but how could they fight something so pervasive? Something his CO had said came to mind: the only battles worth fighting are those you can't win.

He now shared it with the others, adding, "I don't know if we can win or not, but we're sure gonna try."

Laurel gave him a grateful smile.

Once again, he thought of Ronnie Winston. They needed to cut off his line of communication. Only then could they take down the organization.

"I think another visit to Winston is in order," Laurel said, apparently on the same wavelength as he was.

"I think you're right."

"Thank you, Rachel," Shelley said. "Keep at it and let us know when you've translated more."

After Rachel departed, Shelley stood and walked to the office safe. "Before you go," she said to Laurel and Mace, "there's something else I want to show you." She pulled the money from the safe and took out a packet of hundred-dollar bills. "As you probably know, the most difficult part of counterfeiting is using the right paper. I believe that each of these bills started as a one-dollar bill, was bleached and then printed as a hundred-dollar bill. It's a common practice. These are some of the best I've seen."

Mace knew that Shelley had worked for the Secret Service before starting S&J. Though the Secret Service was now under the Department of Homeland Security, Shelley had no doubt learned about counterfeiting techniques from her contacts at the Treasury Department.

"How did you know?" he asked.

"If you look carefully, you'll see that the printing on the bills is slightly off centered. It takes an incredible amount of patience and talent to position the engraving machine on individual bills. If you didn't know what you were looking for, you'd probably miss it."

"The whole lot of them is counterfeit?" Laurel asked.

"I haven't had the time to go through all of them, but my guess is yes. I think this is the endgame, to flood the Southeast with funny money. The resulting chaos will give the Collective the opportunity to put more people in its pocket and to seize control of the economy.

"I've got a friend at Treasury," Shelley continued. "He's arranged for you to meet with Roberto

Calzone, an agent who specializes in counterfeiting. Tell him what we've discovered. Show him the money." She handed the packet of bills to Mace.

"We can visit Winston another day," he said. "I doubt we could have seen him today anyway, what with the hoops Shelley had to jump through the last time to get us in."

Laurel nodded. "You're right." She turned to Shelley. "Okay if I leave Sammy here? He's been cooped up in the cabin all alone. I think he'd like to be with you and Jake rather than go with us to a stuffy government office."

"Fine by me." Shelley patted her leg. "Come here, boy. You and I can get better acquainted."

Mace reviewed what Shelley had just told them. This whole thing was bigger than he ever expected. For the first time, he doubted his ability to keep Laurel safe. For the first time, he doubted himself.

SIXTEEN

Laurel went over all she'd learned about the Collective. It came back to Winston. He hadn't struck her as particularly intelligent. So how was he able to devise a system so complex that he could communicate with the outside without tripping any of the safeguards in place to monitor him?

Maybe he wasn't.

She chewed on it and felt the shift and slide of pieces falling into place. Was she on to something? She recalled working on a jigsaw puzzle she'd dug out of the neighbors' trash when she was ten. The pieces refused to fit until she looked at them from a different angle. Was that what she needed now? To look at the problem from a different perspective?

The warden had insisted that Winston couldn't be involved. At the time, Laurel and Mace had dismissed that, believing that the man was deceiving himself out of a certainty that nothing could get by when he was in charge. Pride had been the root of more than one man's downfall.

But what if Winston wasn't the one running the operation? What if he was only a figurehead? What if someone else, someone close to him, was the true head of the Collective?

The idea circled in her head. The more she thought about it, the more it made sense. Winston hadn't given off a vibe of great intelligence. On the contrary, he seemed of average intellectual ability, if that. He had a blustering bravado, but she hadn't seen anything to make her believe that he had the leadership skills, much less the intellectual horsepower, to run a vast organization.

But, if not Winston, then who was giving the orders? One of his lieutenants? That was the only thing that made sense, but something still didn't feel right. She recalled something she'd picked up from a neighbor's garage sale years back. A chess set. Laurel had taught herself to play. One maxim had stood out. The queen held the power.

Jenni-Grace?

Laurel shook her head in answer to her unspoken question. The woman came from money, had the requisite breeding and background to earn her a place on the boards of numerous charities, even when her image had been tarnished by her marriage to Ronnie Winston. No way could she be involved.

Mace threw her a quick look. "What's going on in that big brain of yours?"

Laurel shook her head. "I'm not sure," she said and told him of her hypothesis.

"Is this a guess or is it your gut talking?"

She didn't have to think about it. "My gut."

"Your gut always knows before your head figures it out. If you're right, we're back at square one."

The depressing thought hung over her as they arrived at the federal building. A quick check of the building's roster gave them the floor and number of Calzone's office.

After introductions had been made, Laurel went through the story of what had brought them there.

"The Collective continues to grow and is infiltrating more and more areas," Mace added. "We think the counterfeiting is part of their endgame. If they control the currency, they control the economy."

"This is indeed troubling," Calzone said, hound-dog wrinkles emphasizing heavy jowls.

The man's response came across as forced to Laurel. The way he spaced the words out caused her to wonder why he was so deliberate in his speech. And why didn't he appear more concerned about the possibility of counterfeit money flooding the Southeast?

Calzone scratched his nose and covered his

mouth in a more or less continuous rhythm, both micro-expressions of lying.

"Thank you for bringing this to my attention. I'll take the money now," he said, holding out a hand. "Don't want it accidentally getting into circulation." The last was said with an attempt at humor. It felt false, as did the rest of his words. Before she could respond, he added, "What about the rest of the bills? It was my understanding that there was approximately ten thousand dollars."

Knowing that they had no legitimate reason to refuse, Laurel reluctantly handed over the pack of hundred-dollar bills. "We'll get the rest of the money to you." She gave him a last doubtful look. "You'll look into this?"

"You can count on it."

She couldn't bring herself to leave. Not yet. "What will you do?"

"We'll handle it. No need to…" He broke off. "It's in the hands of Treasury now."

She feared he'd been about to say 'No need to worry your pretty head over it,' as so many men had said in the past. If he had, she couldn't have spoken to his safety.

Just as she and Mace were about to leave, Laurel noticed that Calzone sported a green tattoo on his wrist. Though she could make out only a portion of the image beneath his shirt cuff, something about it triggered a memory.

On their way back to S&J headquarters to report on the meeting, Laurel said, "Something's off about Calzone."

"How do you mean?"

"He didn't seem very upset about the fact that the Collective is counterfeiting money. In fact, he didn't even seem surprised."

"Yeah, I picked up on that, too. Wonder why."

Could Calzone be one of the organization's plants? According to Rachel's translation of the ledger, dozens of people in Atlanta were implicated in the Collective. Why not Calzone?

And then there was his tattoo. She'd finally placed it. Unless she was very much mistaken, it was a match to the one Dresden sported. She was about to say as much to Mace when two motorcycles appeared behind the truck.

With powerful engines, twin Ducatis closed in on Mace and Laurel from either side. These were obviously no low-level foot soldiers, but lieutenants or even higher-ups in the Collective hierarchy.

They would have to be to afford such expensive motorcycles. One of the motorcyclists aimed a gun and took a shot. Fortunately, he missed the tire, but it didn't matter. A tractor trailer barreled toward Mace and Laurel, the rumble of its huge engine deafening as the vehicle was nearly upon them, the acrid scent of diesel heavy in the air.

"Hold on," Mace said. "We're going to take a hit."

A hit didn't begin to describe the tractor trailer's massive weight plowing into their truck, sending it spinning. Their vehicle did a one-eighty before flipping over.

When she got her breath back, Laurel looked around for Mace and didn't see him. Had he been thrown clear of the truck? Slowly, with every movement sending shafts of pain through her, she undid her seat belt and extricated herself from where she was wedged between the airbag and the seat. She spied Mace lying on the pavement.

When she started toward him, she saw a black-clad man coming at him. She drew her weapon and fired, and the man dropped to the ground.

Laurel ran to bend over Mace. A gash on his forehead was bleeding profusely. She tore a sleeve from her shirt to press against the wound. Bruising hands lifted her off the ground, causing her to drop her weapon.

She whipsawed her arms, breaking the man's hold, and, in the next second, kicked out backward, planting the sole of her foot flat against his chest. He floundered for a moment before slamming to the pavement.

There was no time for self-congratulations as he instantly jumped to his feet and turned to face her, his mouth twisted in an ugly parody of a smile.

"You shouldna done that, girlie," he said.

She didn't waste time answering and braced herself for the next attack.

She'd noticed that before each attack, he wet his lips. He did so now, his intention as clear as a neon sign. He came in low, using his head as a battering ram. She knew if he got her to the ground, it was all over.

Just as he would have hit her, she twisted to the side. His momentum carried him to the ground. When he picked himself up this time, rage distorted his features. He probably wasn't accustomed to being bested.

He wiped his mouth with the back of his hand, and she understood that the preliminaries were over. She was in for the fight of her life. If only she could reach her piece, but it lay two feet away. It might as well be two miles for all the good it did her.

He made a move to the right, and she did the same. Mirroring his moves might confuse him. It seemed to have worked, for he paused, looked about as though trying to understand why she'd done the opposite of what he'd expected.

The driver climbed down from the semi. "Keep it up and your friend's dead," he said, aiming a modified MP5 at Mace's head. The 9mm submachine gun was a lot of weapon. If the man fired, Mace would be killed.

It was that simple. And so was her choice.

Instantly, she went still.

"Good move."

Mace hadn't moved. Blood continued to seep from the wound at his temple.

"You two are worse than useless," the driver said to the man who remained standing. "You can't even take down a lone woman."

"She's not just any woman," the other man tossed back. "She's a Ranger, man. You try taking her on."

"She's a woman," the driver said insultingly. "Quit whining and take care of her."

The other man zip-tied her hands behind her and tossed her into the truck. He then proceeded to hog-tie her, looping a length of rope from her hands to her feet, and placed a cloth hood over her head. She fought it, feeling helpless without the sense of sight, but her struggle was futile.

She had to depend upon her hearing to know what the men were doing. A bounce on the trailer bed told her that the man must have hopped down. Another commotion ensued.

"He's done for." She recognized the driver's voice. "No sense putting a hood on him."

Mace.

The sound of metal scraping against metal followed. She deduced that the men had put the motorcycles in the trailer and secured them somehow.

"Mace, can you hear me?" she asked after the men had closed the door to the semi's trailer.

Not even a grunt.

Laurel kept her chin up. Not because she was trying to prove something, but because she'd discovered if she did so, she avoided having it bang against the bed of the truck. She tried rolling to her side only to find it was next to impossible.

The position was an extremely awkward one, designed to cause her as much pain as possible. Her shoulder screamed in agony with every bounce and shudder of the vehicle. Laurel gave up the struggle to hold back the tears and let them roll down her cheek unchecked.

But she wasn't beaten. The words of a favorite scripture came to mind. *I can do everything through Him who gives me strength.*

"Mace? Mace, do you hear me?" she asked again. She willed Mace to regain consciousness. "Please wake up."

Only silence greeted her.

With nothing she could do at the moment, Laurel considered what had happened, going over her and Mace's steps that had brought them to this place. A visit to Jenni-Grace Winston, a meeting at S&J and then the meeting with Calzone.

The men on the motorcycles and the truck driver had known her and Mace's location. Obviously they'd been set up. Again. There were no tracking devices on them; she and Mace had made sure of that. So where did that leave them?

Calzone. He could easily have called the men who had staged the attack, told them when and where she and Mace would be.

They were in a tight spot, with no weapons and with Mace likely concussed.

She squared her shoulders as much as she was able, considering she was trussed up like a Thanksgiving turkey.

The tractor trailer growled to a stop. It took several minutes for the vibrations to settle. Laurel braced herself. Another minute passed before someone opened the door, grabbed the rope tying her hands to her feet and yanked her out of the truck and onto the hard ground. The hood was pulled away.

Calzone was there waiting. "Looking a little worse for wear," he observed. He cut the rope binding her hands and feet, allowing her to stand, then directed a man to cuff her hands.

"Do his as well," Calzone ordered, pointing to Mace. "We're not risking these two getting free."

She managed a quick look around as she got her bearings. The camp was divided into sections according to function: a cook area, a sleep area, and a weapons area. All in all, it was a neatly arranged compound, self-sustaining and efficient.

"Nothing to say for yourself?" the Treasury agent taunted.

Mouth full of dirt and gravel, Laurel didn't

bother answering, all her thoughts on Mace. "Please…get him out. Let me see to his head."

Two men dragged Mace from the truck, let him fall to the ground. Hands still bound, Laurel attempted to kneel beside him before she was pulled roughly to her feet.

"Not so fast," Calzone said.

"He's hurt."

"It hardly matters. If he's not dead yet, he will be soon enough. As will you."

She shook off his hands. "I knew you were dirty."

"You had no idea that I was working the other side. How could you?"

"The tattoo. I saw the same one on Dresden." She raised her voice. "Dresden, come on out. I know you're there."

After some shuffling in the background, Dresden appeared.

"Might as well show her your tattoo," Calzone said. "She already knows."

Both men rolled up their sleeves to reveal intricately drawn hydras, the serpentine water monster of Greek and Roman mythology. She called up what she remembered from school about the hydra. It had nine heads; when one was cut off, two more appeared.

A perfect symbol for the Collective. When one member was taken out, two others took his place.

No wonder it wielded so much power while inspiring an equal amount of fear.

"It was you who set us up after our visit to the prison," Laurel said to Dresden, not bothering to mask the contempt in her voice. "Tell me, what does it take to commit treason against your country? A vacation home in Maui. Or perhaps the Bahamas. A Bentley. Or maybe a Rolls Royce."

"If I didn't do it, someone would have," the warden said without a trace of shame. "There was so much money. Unbelievable money. Why shouldn't I get my share of it? I worked in that cruddy prison for twenty years and I still don't make more than what the Collective pays me in one week. So, yeah, why shouldn't I get something more for myself and my family?"

"Oh, I don't know. Maybe because you're supposed to keep the bad guys in jail, not join them."

"Like I said, somebody else would have taken the job. And I'd have ended up with my throat cut. Or worse. And what about my family? I had to protect my wife and children. The Collective prides itself on taking out the families of its enemies. And what they do isn't pretty." Self-righteousness filled his voice.

She might have believed him if not for the greed in his eyes when he'd spoken of the money involved. "If you were in danger, you could have gone to the authorities and gotten protection. For you and your family."

Dresden made a scoffing sound. "Who would you suggest? How could I know that anyone I went to wasn't on the take as well? They'd cut my throat before I could get two words out."

The man had a point, but that didn't excuse conspiring to commit murder.

"And greed had nothing to do with it, did it?" Laurel asked. "You could have found a way to refuse and protect your family. You just didn't want to. You were much more interested in ingratiating yourself with the real head of the Collective."

She thought she had the answer, but she wanted to hear what Dresden had to say. "Winston's the head. Everybody knows that."

"Oh, I don't think so. I don't think Winston has the smarts to run the Collective. And I know you and Calzone don't. You're both yes men. You're too afraid of your own shadows to do anything that requires real planning."

Calzone bristled at that. "So who is it?" he asked in the tone of one who believed she didn't have a clue.

"It's the last person anyone would suspect. The person who's remained in the background. The person who could visit Winston in prison without drawing attention. The person who could carry back supposed orders from Winston.

"You might as well come out, Jenni-Grace,"

Laurel said, raising her voice. "I know you're there. You wouldn't want to miss this."

Exiting a tent, the woman sauntered into view carrying a rifle. "I was afraid you'd figured it out. How did you know?"

"I had to ask myself why a woman like you would have anything to do with the likes of Ronnie Winston. Why would you lower yourself to even give him the time of day, much less marry him?"

"Now why would I go and do something like that? As you say, I'm a classy society lady." Jenni-Grace made air quotes around the words.

"Because you saw something in him. A kind of charisma that you could turn to your own ends. You were playing a long game, content to watch him take center stage while you appeared the dutiful, if somewhat dimwitted, wife."

"Right the first time," Jenni-Grace said, reluctant admiration in her voice. "I met Ronnie when I was twenty-five. He was ten years older, but he was going nowhere. Still, I saw his potential. He had a way of talking that made people want to listen. I knew I could use that."

"You used him just like you used these two." Laurel gestured to the two men. "They're like Ronnie. They're weak, don't have the brains to do anything on their own, but I'm guessing they knew how to obey orders."

Both Calzone and Dresden took umbrage at

the unflattering description. "You can't say that about us," Dresden said, all indignation and puffed-up pride.

"Shut up," Jenni-Grace ordered. "She's right. You two don't have the brains to blow your own noses unless I tell you to. Fortunately, I didn't bring you into the Collective because of your brains."

Calzone threw back his shoulders, while Dresden continued to sputter.

"Don't be going all macho on me," she told them. "You're both weak, but you have your uses. That's why I recruited you. You'll continue to do as I say when I say it. You wouldn't want to disobey me. You know what happens to those foolish enough to do so."

Both men shrank from the menace in her voice.

"She'll turn on you," Laurel said to them. "Both of you. When you're of no further use to her, she'll get rid of you. Same as she'll get rid of Ronnie when he ceases to be useful. No doubt she has others in the wings who can take your place."

"Don't listen to her," Jenni-Grace ordered the two men. "Or you'll find yourself like that judge from a while back."

Laurel recoiled in horror at the woman's casual mention of murder. "You need help. Ordering the deaths of anyone who stands in your way and their families is sick."

Twisted pride gleamed in the other woman's eyes. "Sick? I call it preventive medicine. The Collective needs to be feared. What better way to do that than to take out its enemies?"

Laurel looked for an opening, any opening, to get the drop on Jenni-Grace, but with her wrists cuffed, she was at a distinct disadvantage.

"You're wondering how you can take me down. Don't bother denying it. I see it in your eyes. I know how you think. I saw it when you paid me a visit this morning. You didn't talk much. You were assessing. My house. My clothes. Me. Wondering how I'd come to marry Ronnie. I could see then that you were going to be a problem.

"You and I have a lot in common. It would be interesting to see how a match between us played out, but I can't risk it. There's too much at stake."

Laurel was repulsed at any comparison between herself and Jenni-Grace, but she let it go. She was too busy thinking of the time that had passed. Had Shelley and Jake figured out that she and Mace were missing? Even if they had, they'd have no idea where she and Mace were being held.

Time was something they were quickly running out of.

* * *

Mace heard the exchange between Laurel and Jenni-Grace. He longed to get to his feet to protect Laurel from the woman's viciousness, but he didn't, though it cost him dearly to remain still.

Two things rendered him silent. First, he was still hovering between unconsciousness and wakefulness. More importantly, he had the advantage of Jenni-Grace and the others not knowing that he had regained consciousness. That might be the only thing he and Laurel had going for them. He had to bide his time.

He listened to Jenni-Grace's bragging and agreed with Laurel. The woman was sick. It had been her all along. Ronnie hadn't used her; it had been the other way around. She had deceived everyone. The ladylike facade was just that. A facade. Her act had been a convincing performance, but an act was all it was.

With the layers peeled back, her true self was exposed. Hers was an ugly and twisted soul. It all made sense now. Ronnie Winston was a puppet, controlled by a master puppeteer. Mace recalled Laurel's theory that Ronnie didn't have the brains to run something as well-organized as the Collective. She'd been right.

Unfortunately, she had come to the truth too late. He hoped it wasn't too late for them as well. He still had things he wanted to say to her, things he needed to say.

Despite everything, Laurel's faith had never shaken. He wished he could claim only a bit of that for himself. Regret that he'd never told her that he loved her swelled within his throat, making it difficult to breathe.

"How did you manage it, making Ronnie and everyone else think that he was the Collective's head?" Laurel asked. She wanted to keep Jenni-Grace talking. Anything to buy time.

"All I had to do was put ideas in his head and make him think they were his. Easy enough, considering that he hasn't had an original thought in his life. Ego took care of the rest. He was a puppet."

"And nobody will be the wiser. Why are you telling me all of this?"

"Because you won't be here to tell anyone else." Jenni-Grace's tone turned accusatory. "I knew that you were smarter than the average fed or reporter who comes sniffing around every so often. You'd have seen the truth sooner or later." She shifted the pearls around her neck and pointed to the emerald clasp shaped like a hydra. "I noticed you looking at this. I've always loved the hydra. The power of it."

"A perfect symbol for the Collective," Laurel agreed. She understood why Jenni-Grace had her brought here rather than having her killed when she and Mace had been run off the road.

"You wanted the ledger and thought I still had it. Too bad."

"Too bad for you, you mean. Unless your people will trade it for you and your friend." Her eyes grew sly. "Of course, once I get the ledger, I won't need to keep you around."

"You've got to see that you can't keep up all the killing. Pretty soon someone is going to catch on that you're behind everything."

In a fraction of a second, Jenni-Grace was once more a well-bred Southern lady, eyes wide and innocent, mouth bowed. "Who's going to suspect me, a genteel lady, of running the Southeast region of the Collective?"

"You're not as smart as you think you are," Laurel said. "People will be looking for us. They know we saw you earlier and will put it together. You'll never get the ledger if you don't let us go.

"You can stop all this. Put an end to the violence. No one else needs to die." The sneer on the woman's face erased whatever else Laurel might have said.

There'd be no remorse from this woman with the hard mouth and even harder eyes. Her heart had turned against any softness or compassion, if it had ever had any in the first place.

"If you give yourself up, you may get a reduced sentence." Laurel was stalling. She knew it.

Jenni-Grace's sly smile confirmed she understood what Laurel was doing. "Give it up. There's no reduced sentence for treason."

"Treason, as in selling weapons to terrorists?"

"Got it in one. Terrorists pay plenty for American weapons to fight America." Her voice hardened. "America won't know what hit her."

"You'd sell out your country?" Even as Laurel asked the question, she realized the foolishness of it. Jenni-Grace had no remorse for anything she'd done.

"Looks like I was wrong about you being smart. You're almost as stupid as your mother. She stole from us, then tried to blackmail us. Plus, she had the ledger and the money. If either ever got out before we'd put our plans in place, it would have ruined everything."

"Of course."

"Sarcasm? Like I said, you're almost as stupid as your mother. She was nothing. Just like you."

She pushed Laurel with the butt of her rifle, causing Laurel to stumble and fall.

Jenni-Grace yanked Laurel up by her hair.

Tiny daggers of misery speared through her scalp. Laurel barely bit back tears at the pain, but she knew something Jenni-Grace didn't. No one was always the smartest person in the room. And no one was invincible.

SEVENTEEN

Laurel asked the question that had been nagging at her. "Why do this? You had money, background, family name." Even in the New South, family name remained all-important.

"Background and family name mean nothing without money." Jenni-Grace made a dismissing motion with her hand as though the subject were of no importance. "If you'd turned over the ledger and money in the first place, you could have saved your life."

"You were never going to let me live. I knew that from the beginning."

Jenni-Grace appeared to consider it. "You're probably right. But you'd turn it over now if it would save your man's life, wouldn't you?" Viciously, she kicked Mace in the kidneys.

Laurel wrested her way free of the men who held her arms, but she couldn't throw herself over Mace without body-slamming him. She glared up at Jenni-Grace. "Leave him alone."

At a fulminating look from their boss, the two men jerked Laurel to her feet.

"Please don't do this. Do what you want to with me, but don't hurt him anymore. Don't kill him. He hasn't seen you, any of you. You're safe to leave him alive." The words scratched at her throat as she thought of what was waiting for her and Mace.

"How touching." The sneer in the woman's voice promised no mercy. "The two of you have caused me no end of trouble by forcing my hand. I'll have to move up the timetable because of it."

Jenni-Grace gave Mace a final kick.

Laurel had witnessed her share of depravity. There were people in the world who fed on cruelty. Jenni-Grace Winston was one of them.

Mace assessed their situation, all the while fighting the need to curl up in a ball of pain and give way to the oblivion of unconsciousness that beckoned. It would have been easy—too easy— to do exactly that. With a probable concussion and his hands bound, he was worse than useless. He fought back the wave of nausea that threatened to overcome him.

Bad didn't begin to describe the danger he and Laurel faced. They were in the clutches of a woman who had no remorse about killing anyone who got in her way.

Laurel had definitely gotten in the way. She'd

stood up to Jenni-Grace without regard for her own life, but she'd pleaded for his unashamedly. Never would he forget her magnificence. Or her selflessness.

His SEREs training—survival, evasion, resistance and escape—was imprinted in his brain from his Ranger training. He had missed the window for evasion, but there was still survival, resistance and escape. He might not be able to escape or to survive, but he'd resist with his last breath. That's what Rangers did.

He wanted to signal Laurel that he was awake, but he didn't want to alert Jenni-Grace or her henchmen.

Patience, he cautioned himself. *Patience.*

Laurel wasn't done yet.

Adapt and overcome. The axiom was drilled into spec-op warriors. She and several of her buddies had adopted the SEAL motto as well— *Never let failure become an option*. It had stood them in good stead during high-stress ops that could easily have gone south.

An inkling of a plan formed in her mind. It might get her killed, but on the other hand, she didn't have a lot to lose. She needed only a heartbeat of distraction. She threw herself at Jenni-Grace and, with her bound hands, grabbed at the woman's hair.

Jenni-Grace screamed and slapped Laurel hard enough that she fell to the ground.

"Hair-pulling? Really? You're a Ranger. I thought you were better than that." Jenni-Grace patted her hair back into place.

"Sorry to disappoint." Blood trickled from Laurel's mouth, but she didn't wipe it away and got to her feet, not an easy feat with her hands cuffed.

Her captors regarded her with varying degrees of distrust and hatred.

"Kill them now," Calzone urged. "We're never going to get our hands on that ledger, and nobody can decode it anyway. I always said you made too much of it when that woman took it."

Dresden sent the other man a withering look. "As long as the ledger and the money are in play, we aren't safe. You're so stupid, it's a wonder you don't shoot yourself with your own gun. I don't know why we recruited you in the first place."

"Because we needed him to distribute the money." Jenni-Grace solved the matter by lifting her rifle to her shoulder. "Too bad we don't need you any longer," she said to Calzone and shot him in the chest.

Calzone fell to the ground.

Laurel gasped.

Even Dresden looked shocked. "I didn't mean—"

"You didn't mean what? That I should take

care of a problem? You said it yourself. He was weak. The Collective needs strength. Keep whining and I'll wonder if you should be eliminated as well."

Dresden backed off. "You're right. He had to go."

Jenni-Grace gave him the same withering glance with which he'd favored Calzone.

"Killing someone doesn't make you strong," Laurel said, unable to hide her revulsion. "It only makes you cruel. Cruel and stupid, because someday you'll have to pay for your actions."

"You're a fool. Women like you are always trying to compete with a man on his terms. I learned a long time ago that women have their own power. We just have to learn to use it."

Ironically, Laurel agreed with her. Too bad that they were on opposite sides. Laurel would always defend those who were weaker and unable to defend themselves, while Jenni-Grace would exploit them for her own advantage.

"You're the fool."

Jenni-Grace slapped her once more. Laurel's head snapped back, but again, she managed to stay on her feet. Barely.

"How do you figure that? From where I'm sitting, I'm the one who holds all the power. I can have you killed with just a word." A sly smile entered her eyes. "Or worse."

Laurel had seen that smile all over the world.

It was the smile of predator to prey. Of a warlord ordering the death of an underling who had disobeyed him. Of an enemy soldier who had violated a young girl. It was the smile Bernice had used when she'd told a nine-year-old Laurel that the only reason she kept her around was for the welfare checks. *Why else would I keep a whiny brat like you?*

Laurel pushed away the memory, stared into Jenni-Grace's eyes, and saw that the smile had grown into something even more sinister. A smile born of malice and power. It announced that Laurel and Mace were as good as dead and that she might as well accept it.

But Laurel refused to cower before it.

"As soon as I get the ledger, you're dead." Jenni-Grace said the words with no great passion, only hard determination.

Regret washed through Laurel. Not at the idea of her own probable death, but that she had not told Mace how she felt about him. He would never know that she loved him with all of her heart.

She started to say the words now, even if he couldn't hear them, but then stopped. Giving voice to her feelings for Mace would only present Jenni-Grace with one more weapon to use against her. A sob filled her throat. She pushed it down.

Laurel lifted her chin. Her cheek throbbed.

Her arms and legs ached from when they were hog-tied in the truck, but she'd never felt so filled with power. "It doesn't matter what you do with me. You won't win because there are other people like me. People who believe. People who won't let you destroy our country and our way of life. They'll fight you and your so-called soldiers."

"People like your friend? He's no use to you. He's out cold and may never wake up." To emphasize her point, Jenni-Grace kicked Mace again. She then spread her arms wide, the gesture both ebullient and mocking at once. "The world is mine for the taking. Your stupid idealism won't stop it. Nothing can stop it."

"You underestimate all the good people who will fight you until you're beaten." *And you overestimate yourself*, Laurel wanted to add, but didn't. No need to invite another slap from a woman so filled with anger that she wanted to destroy anyone who didn't believe as she did. "What's more, you underestimate the Lord."

Jenni-Grace laughed, a sound of derision and disgust. "Where is your Lord right now? You're dead. You just don't know it yet. But you will. Just as soon as I get the ledger." The look she sent Laurel burned with hatred. "If you don't have the ledger, I'm guessing your pals at S&J do. Yes," she said at Laurel's shock that Jenni-Grace knew of S&J. "I know who they are. Dresden filled me in. Maybe I'll cut off your finger and send it back to them. A little proof that we have you. Put them in a tent," she told Dresden, "and station some men outside."

Jerry and another man carried Mace into a tent, with Dresden pushing Laurel along behind them.

Laurel accepted that she might well die before the sun rose but felt oddly at peace. If she died in doing what was right, she'd know she had given her best. That was all she could ask of herself. More importantly, it was all that God asked of her.

That didn't mean she was going down without a fight.

EIGHTEEN

"I'm awake." Mace spoke softly so as to not attract the attention of the guards stationed outside the tent.

"Mace?" Laurel's voice was filled with confusion...and hope.

"I played dead. I didn't want them to know I could hear what was going on. I've never been more proud of you, Laurel. You stared her down." Despite everything, Laurel's faith had never shaken.

"I managed to get something." She held out a hairpin.

Baffled at first, he simply stared at the pin. Then he understood. "That's why you pulled Jenni-Grace's hair. You had me wondering there for a minute."

"Got it in one. We're getting out of here."

Laurel never gave up.

He wished he could believe her. He wished he could believe the Lord heard his prayers. He wanted to turn to the Lord he'd once believed in, the Lord Laurel held so dear, but what could he say? *Sorry I stopped believing, but I need Your help now.* The Lord would most surely reject such a hypocritical plea.

Mace knew he was the worst kind of unbeliever. He'd been a devout worshipper at one time, but he'd turned away because he couldn't find forgiveness for himself. What was it Laurel had told him? *The Lord forgives everyone, even the very people who crucified Him.*

But love could make a man do the unexpected, and he tried a silent prayer in his mind. The words refused to come, though, having grown rusty with disuse.

Laurel managed to work the hairpin with her bound hands, twisting it in the mechanism of the handcuffs to trip the lock. If ever she needed divine intervention, it was now.

She maneuvered the pin back and forth. When she heard a small click, she wanted to cheer. The cuffs dropped away. She did the same with those shackling Mace.

Okay. Their hands were free. That didn't mean she and Mace could walk away. Still, she flashed a grin at him. "Jenni-Grace and her men are no match for us."

"Like I said, you're Ranger-strong." Mace's

grin was jaunty, but the glazed look in his eyes said that he was far from being a hundred percent.

"We both are."

Despite the brave words, she wasn't blind to the realities. Two Rangers against Jenni-Grace and her men. No problem. Except that the bad guys were armed with semiautomatic weapons and she and Mace didn't have a weapon between them. Except that her shoulder felt like it was on fire, while Mace had a concussion and probably a couple broken ribs from Jenni-Grace's vicious kicks. Except for all that, sure, no problem.

Her self-directed sarcasm didn't help. She had to do something or she and Mace were both dead.

They had known each other for such a short time, not even a week, but she felt as though she'd loved him forever. He filled the empty spaces inside of her, and she prayed she did the same for him. What if she never had the opportunity to tell him? Did she have the courage to tell him that she loved him? What was she waiting for? Things could not have been more dire for them. She started to do just that when he broke the silence between them.

"Laurel, if this is it—"

She didn't give him the opportunity to finish. "Do. Not. Go. There. We're not beaten. Not yet. Someone told me that the only battles worth fighting were those you can't win. Well, we're still fighting."

Yes, but for how long?

With his and Laurel's hands free, Mace judged it time to take on the two guards posted outside the tent. A look-see under the tent's flap had him motioning to Laurel, who nodded in understanding.

Both men had AR-15s hanging across their chests. Impressive weapons, but difficult to bring to bear quickly.

Mace had no desire to give the men the opportunity to fire the assault rifles, thereby alerting the camp, and decided upon a more subtle approach. He slipped from beneath the flap of the tent and took out the first of the men with a chop to the back of the neck.

Laurel did the same with the other guard, then grabbed the handcuffs from which she and Mace had just freed themselves and used them to secure the men's hands. Together, she and Mace dragged the men inside the tent.

When they crept outside again, Dresden and Jerry, the driver, were waiting for them.

"Jenni-Grace says not to kill you," Dresden said. "Yet. Doesn't mean we can't hurt you real bad, though." He clocked Mace behind the ear with a weighted club hard enough to cause him to see stars. Instinctively, Mace protected his head and managed to put enough space between them to give him leverage.

The warden slapped the club against his hand. "Makes a nice sound, doesn't it?"

Dresden had at least fifty pounds on Mace. Now he wrapped his arms around Mace, lifting him off his feet and slamming him face-first into the ground. Still groggy and not yet back to full speed, Mace didn't have the luxury of catching his breath.

His courageous Laurel fought like the warrior she was. She didn't give an inch in her battle with Jerry, finally throwing him to the ground in a back flip. When he started to get up, she bent over and plowed a balled-up fist at his jaw.

He stayed down.

Dresden reared back, leg poised to kick Mace in the ribs. At the last moment, Mace rolled to the side, catching his opponent's foot and yanking him to the ground. He grabbed the warden's gun and held it on him while getting to his feet.

Jenni-Grace stepped out from another tent, took in the situation, and sent Dresden a look of disgust. "All you had to do was keep an eye on the prisoners. Can't you do one thing right?" The rage-filled words ripped like a scalpel through the night.

"They got the drop on the guards," Dresden said, scrambling to his feet and shooting Mace a glare filled with venom. "Guards *you* chose, by the way."

"Give it up, Jenni-Grace," Mace ordered. "You're done. And so is the Collective."

Jenni-Grace pulled something from behind her back. Metal glinted in the moonlight. A .45. Before she could pull the trigger, Laurel threw herself in front of Mace.

"No!" She took two shots, one to her shoulder and another to her chest.

Though Mace had never before hit a woman, he knocked out Jenni-Grace, then kicked her gun out of the way. "I know you have a phone," he said to Dresden. "Call 911. Put it on speaker so I can hear you. Make a wrong move, and you'll regret it."

Part of him was acting on rote; another part was terrified for Laurel.

Dresden did as instructed, giving the location of the camp, and, at Mace's order, asking for a flight-for-life copter.

Mace then rattled off the number for S&J headquarters. "Call them, give them the location and tell them that Laurel's down. Then take a pair of handcuffs and cuff yourself to your boss." He didn't trust himself to say Jenni-Grace's name.

He looked about the camp for any other threats and saw that the few remaining men had scattered. They'd be picked up soon enough once help arrived. With one eye on Dresden, Mace ripped off his sweatshirt, leaving him clad in a black T-shirt, pressed it against Laurel's chest, then tore strips from it and wrapped them around her shoulder.

Blood slicked his hands. Her blood.

The night cold seeped into his bare arms, but he scarcely noticed. All he could think about was Laurel.

As he stared down at the woman he loved, his heart stopped beating. "Don't leave me. Please don't leave me."

He didn't realize he was shouting the words until a part of him registered that someone was shouting and that someone was him.

Focus, Ransom. His fingers probed the delicate column of her neck, found a pulse. Yes! She was alive. Her pulse was faint, but it was there. Definitely there.

But it was growing weaker, and Mace felt the life slipping from her. He willed her to live. Laurel was a fighter. Why wasn't she fighting this? They had fought side by side many times in the past. They could do it again. If only she'd open her eyes…

The Lord is always there. Laurel's words filled his mind. There, in the midst of the Collective's camp, with chaos going on around him, he prayed. He didn't stop applying pressure to Laurel's wounds. Nor did he take his eyes off

Dresden and Jenni-Grace. He continued to pray and to listen.

Nothing.

Laurel had been wrong. The Lord might answer the prayers of others, but He wasn't going to give Mace the time of day. He thought of her faith and her certainty that the Lord would never desert him, no matter the circumstances.

Okay, I get it. You have better things to do than to talk with me. I'm about as far from perfect as you can get. But Laurel... Laurel's good and decent and she's in trouble.

"I love her, Lord. Please save her. You're the only one who can."

Love. Tentatively, Mace tasted the word on his lips. He'd used it without thinking, but it tasted right. Felt right. He was in love with Laurel. She was infuriating. Courageous. Loyal to a fault. She was all that and more. And he loved her with his whole being.

If he lost her... No. He refused to go there.

Guilt lapped at him, a nagging reminder that he'd failed to tell her of his feelings. If he had, would it have made a difference?

NINETEEN

Laurel was drifting. Waiting, she supposed, for the loss of blood to overtake her and drain the life from her. Red mist, edged with black, crawled across her vision. Regret whispered through her. She'd found the man she hadn't known she was looking for, and now it was too late.

In the last days, there'd been little time for personal exchanges, or for anything except surviving.

Aside from the sorrow that Mace would never know how she felt about him, her biggest regret was that she had too few memories of their time together. They'd had only several brief days with each other, and those days were packed with taking on bad guys multiple times, having their truck rammed into a river and facing Jenni-Grace and her henchman in a final showdown.

But there had been sweet times as well, such as Mace kissing her outside the prison, the moment shimmering with color, sound and taste.

She held on to that image, but it kept fading. Why did it insist upon disappearing?

Was it because another question was pushing itself forward?

The question took center stage. Had anything she'd done in her life mattered? Yes, she'd served her country to the best of her ability. Yes, she'd served the Lord, once more to the best of her ability. Perhaps that's all that really mattered.

Never give up.

But how could she fight the inevitable? She was bleeding at an alarming rate. Already, she could feel her heart slow, her mind shutting down, the life leaking from her.

"Laurel!"

She heard Mace's voice from a great distance. Or had she? How could she know when her mind kept taking detours? There was something she wanted to tell him. She remembered now. She wanted to tell him that she loved him and always would. Maybe she already had. She couldn't remember.

After a moment's consideration, she decided she had. He'd been unconscious then, but she'd said the words. Strange to think that uttering those few words had taken more courage than staring down Jenni-Grace.

With the part of her brain that was still functioning, Laurel held on to that as well as the fact that her faith hadn't faltered. Even with the knowledge that she would probably die from the gunshot wounds, her belief had remained intact. The Lord would be proud of her. He would greet her with open arms. He would...

"Laurel. Come back to me. You have to come back. Now!"

Was that Mace's voice again?

Why was he yelling at her? What had she done to deserve that? She tried to tell him that she didn't care for it, but she couldn't find the words.

"Don't leave me." His voice lowered to a murmur. "Please don't leave me. I don't deserve you. But I need you. I need you more than I've ever needed anything or anyone."

It's okay, she said. But the words failed to materialize. She tried again. And once again, couldn't get the words out.

Gentle arms cradled her.

Yes, that felt good. So good. She wished she could tell him that. She hoped he knew.

"I can't lose you."

Oh, my dearest Mace, I can't lose you either. And Sammy. Maybe they'd take care of each other. With that thought, she allowed the beckoning blackness to claim her.

"No!" Mace shouted the word. Or he thought he did. He could barely hear it over the roar of his heart. "Laurel..." Fear got a chokehold around his lungs, making it impossible to breathe. He forced out a breath, looked at Laurel.

Her eyes had glazed over, her mouth slack. He felt for a pulse. Couldn't find one. He'd gladly trade his life for hers. He registered the arrival of vehicles and heard a helicopter hovering overhead. "Over here," he yelled. "I need help. Now."

Hurried footsteps. Hands prying him away from Laurel. Urgent voices.

"Mace, let us help her." Mace tried to place the voice. Jake's?

"The EMTs are here." He heard Shelley's voice as well. "Mace, let them see to Laurel. She'll be taken care of as soon as you let her go. I know you want to hold her, but you need to let them do their job."

Mace stopped resisting and allowed the medics to take Laurel.

Someone saw to his wounds. "That's a nasty graze on your arm," a young EMT said. Mace looked at his arm in surprise. He hadn't even felt the sting of the bullet. The EMT applied antiseptic and pressed gauze over the wound at his temple and the graze on his arm, but Mace scarcely noticed.

How could he when every thought was with Laurel? Her courage had saved his life.

He saw her being lifted into a medevac chopper and tried to get to her.

"Let her go," Jake said. "They'll take care of her."

"I need to go with her." Once more, Mace made to start after her but was stopped with a large hand to his chest.

"You're in no condition to go anywhere on your own." Jake gestured to Mace's head wound, which had started to bleed again.

Two EMTs helped him into an ambulance.

Mace felt every jolt of the ambulance as it bumped over the rough ground. He was grateful for the pain, as it reminded him that he was still alive. When he'd seen Laurel take those bullets—bullets meant for him—he'd thought his heart had stopped beating.

Prayers circled through his mind. *Lord, take care of her. I failed her. I know I've got no right coming to You now after ignoring You for so many years, but I'm begging for Laurel's life. That has to count for something. I've never begged before, but I am now. Laurel says that You hear every prayer, even from sinners like me. So please listen to this one.*

He finished the prayer and felt a measure of peace.

As though he were emerging from a fog, he got out of the transport vehicle under his own steam. The EMTs tried to assist him, but he waved off their help.

At the hospital, Mace was whisked away to a

cubicle. He hated the smell of hospitals, a stale antiseptic odor that stank of overripe flowers and despair.

An efficient-looking nurse pushed her way through the drawn curtains and began to examine his wounds.

He pushed aside the nurse's hands. "I've got to get to Laurel. She's my…" He searched for the right word to describe her. "She's my partner." She was also the love of his life, but he didn't think the nurse cared about that.

"She'll be taken care of. In the meantime, it's my job to take care of you. You have a nasty gash on your head. It looks like someone pressed a cloth to it, but it's bleeding through." She nodded, drawing his attention to the blood-soaked gauze the EMT had applied. "So is your arm."

"I was knocked out for a while. I probably have a concussion. Nothing serious."

"Anything that starts with a bullet and ends with a concussion is serious. Now lie back and let me see to you. Or I can have two orderlies come in and hold you down. Condition you're in, you couldn't fight off a newborn kitten."

She was right. The sooner he submitted to her ministrations, the faster he could see Laurel. He gritted his teeth. "Do what you have to."

He scarcely felt the prick of the IV needle; nor did he feel the nurse poking around at his arm or seeing to his head.

"You'll have to have an MRI for your head."

"I don't have time."

"You'll make time." With a beehive hairdo, a build like a Sherman tank and arms folded over a massive chest, she looked like she could take on two Ranger units by herself and come out on top.

"Okay."

"That's better."

He was wheeled to the room where the magnetic resonance imaging would take place.

A technician appeared shortly. "Let's get this done."

Mace couldn't have agreed more.

"You have a concussion." The technician took in Mace's battered face and body. "But you already knew that."

Mace refrained, barely, from saying "Told you so" to the nurse. That wouldn't earn him any points.

She took him back to the cubicle. Finally, she appeared to be finished with him. "We're going to give you something to help you sleep." She pulled a syringe from a metal cart and plunged it into an IV tube.

Sleep? Was the woman crazy? He needed to see to Laurel. "How is she?" he managed to ask before the nurse plunged the needle into his arm.

"You'll find out once you've rested."

He tried to push her away, found that he couldn't.

"What did I tell you? You're as weak as a new-born kitten. And not nearly as cute."

His last thought was of Laurel when he closed his eyes. He had a feeling that every thought for the rest of his life would be of her.

He slept, though he had no idea of how long. He awoke to find a doctor standing over him, examining his chart.

"How long have I been out?" His mouth was dry, and he had to try a couple of times before he could get the words out.

"Six hours."

Six hours? How could that be? He'd just closed his eyes for a moment, hadn't he?

Mace waved away the doctor's attempt to comment on his own condition and asked about Laurel.

"I'm sorry. I can't give out that information to someone who isn't family."

"Please. I'm the reason she's here in the first place."

The doctor looked undecided, then his face cleared. "As I said, I can't give out that information, but if I could, I'd say that Ms. Landry should pull through. She has a nasty hole in her shoulder and another in her chest, but we've removed the bullets." He shook his head. "I'm no expert, but I'd say bigger than a 9mm. Probably a .45 caliber." Another shake of his head.

Mace marshaled his thoughts. "What about

her shoulder?" He wet his lips. "She was hit by shrapnel overseas and was doing PT for it here at home."

"I saw the damage." The doctor's voice had gentled. "I understand Ms. Landry was a Ranger."

The use of the past tense wasn't lost on Mace.

"That's right," he said. "Will she…" He knew the answer before he got out the rest of the words, but he had to ask. "Will she be able to return to her unit?"

"An Army doctor will have to make that determination, but I'm guessing not. Not with the damage her shoulder had already sustained and that of last night."

"Thank you, doctor."

"Don't thank me. I heard that you were the one who put pressure on the wounds and staunched the blood. You saved her life with that."

Mace didn't deserve any credit. Laurel had saved his life with her heroic actions. Saved his life and cost her any possibility of returning to the Rangers.

He sank back against the mattress, giving himself a minute to take in what the doctor had told him. Relief that she would live rolled through him, quickly followed by a wave of guilt.

It wouldn't be the first time he'd had to live with paralyzing guilt. It probably wouldn't be the last. He tried to wrap his mind around that.

No good. The guilt didn't want to stay wrapped in a tidy bundle.

The curtain was pulled back. Jake, Shelley and Caleb stepped inside the cubicle. "You up for visitors?" Jake asked.

The last thing he wanted to do was to see his friends. They had to be blaming him just as he was blaming himself for what had happened to Laurel. But all he said was, "Sure. Come on in."

Shelley's eyes were filled with concern, as were those of Jake and Caleb. "You gave us a scare," she said.

"I'm fine." To prove it, he reached for the IV needle in an attempt to rip it out.

Jake pushed his hand away. "Don't be stupid."

"I want to see Laurel."

"She's still in recovery," Shelley said gently.

"I want to see her."

"When the doctor says she's ready." Caleb favored Mace with a critical look. "No offense, buddy, but you look like the south end of a northbound mule."

"I'm afraid he's right, Mace," Shelley added.

Jake nodded. "You don't want to scare Laurel looking like you do now." He held out a sack. "We stopped by your place and picked up some clothes for you. When you're able to, you can change into something besides that hospital gown. Though you do look mighty cute in it."

Mace tried to growl at his friend's teasing,

but unfortunately, it came out more like a kitten's mewl.

Jake and Shelley chuckled; a few seconds later, Mace joined in.

"Where's Sammy?"

"At our place," Shelley answered, "with Tommy, Chloe and the nanny. He's in good hands."

Relieved that Sammy was being well cared for, he nodded. It couldn't be put off any longer. "Have you talked with her doctor?"

Shelley's expression turned serious. "Yes. He said that Laurel will be all right."

"Did he tell you the rest?" Mace tensed. Here it came, the blame they would heap upon him. Blame he richly deserved.

"About her probably not being able to return to the Rangers? Yes." Shelley took his hand. "She's strong. She can live with that. The important thing is that she'll live." She gave his hand a little shake. "Do you hear that? She'll live."

There was no blame in her voice, nor in her eyes or those of his buddies.

"She'll live," Shelley repeated. "That's all that matters."

Mace held on to that.

"The doctor also said that you probably saved her life," Shelley added, "staunching the blood the way you did."

* * *

Three hours later, he felt a hand on his shoulder. "Mr. Ransom, you can see your friend now."

See Laurel? He made to get up.

The nurse pushed a wheelchair forward. "You'll need this."

"I'm fine to walk."

"You're recovering from a concussion and a bullet wound."

"Graze," he corrected automatically.

"You *will* use the wheelchair." Her voice brooked no argument. She helped him into the wheelchair, pushed him down a corridor and into Laurel's room. "You have fifteen minutes. I'll leave the door open. Call if you need something."

The room was dimly lit. Monitors coughed and burped, registering vitals and spitting out information.

Mace let his eyes look their fill. She was pale. So pale. But he could see the quiet up-and-down movement of her chest, hear the soft wisp of her breathing. She'd be all right. As Shelley had said, that was all that mattered.

Shaking with the realization of what he'd almost lost, he let his head hang, braced his hands on his legs and worked to steady his breathing.

He didn't hear the beep and whistle of the machines attached to Laurel. He didn't hear the pad of rubber-soled shoes as they whispered over the linoleum floor. Nor did he hear the murmur of voices that buzzed behind him.

All he heard was the even sound of Laurel's breathing. Everything else was just noise. There, in the hospital room, he prayed. He didn't care who heard. Except for God. He hoped the Lord listened.

"Lord, thank You for giving Laurel back to me. Thank You. I don't deserve Your love, but she does."

He took a final look at her. Love filled him. He wheeled himself out of the room without glancing back.

Laurel was better off without him.

Laurel felt herself floating. Her thoughts hazed as she went in and out of consciousness. Had she heard someone praying? She wasn't certain. How much time had passed?

An hour? A day?

She tried to remember where she was. She'd heard voices, commanding and urgent, calm and desperate mixed together. With a mighty effort, she managed to open her eyes momentarily and looked up to see a ceiling she didn't recognize.

She would have laughed at herself if she'd been able, wondering about an unfamiliar ceiling. It took too much effort to keep her eyes open, and she felt them close. There, that was better.

More voices moved in and out of her hearing

range. One stood out from the others. It was calling her name. Why wouldn't her brain work? She managed to open her eyes for a nanosecond and registered tubes hooked up to her arm, another kind of tube in her mouth.

Her mouth and throat were unbearably dry. Was she in a hospital? She tried to focus. She'd been shot. Mace! Was he all right? Why couldn't she remember? If she'd had the strength, she would have ripped out the tubes and found him.

At some point, she'd lifted her head and seen him. At least she thought she had. She struggled to replay the scene in her mind. Slowly, it came into focus.

She'd looked up to find his gaze resting on her. Softly. Gently.

"M…"

"Shh. Don't talk. I'm here."

He didn't say anything more, only continued looking at her. The warmth in his eyes had wrapped her in a cocoon of safety. Why didn't he say anything more? She longed to hear his voice, to know he was all right.

So tired. Her eyes closed. When she opened them again, he was gone. Hours had passed. Or maybe it was minutes. She couldn't tell. Nurses came and went, checking on the tubes that hooked her to machines. One pointed a bright light in her eyes. She didn't like that, tried to tell the nurse to stop doing it, but her words came out garbled.

"You're doing just fine, Ms. Landry," an unfamiliar voice said. "Doctor says you'll make a full recovery."

"G…good." Laurel tried out her voice and was grateful to find it was working this time. She looked about for Mace. She'd hoped…prayed… he'd be there when she woke up.

"Mace?" she asked. "Mace Ransom. Is he here?"

"Mr. Ransom was released yesterday."

"Yesterday?"

"That's right."

"Do you know if he came to see me?" Laurel heard the plea in her voice, but she had to know.

"I wouldn't know. I've just been on duty for the last eight hours. But I heard someone say that Mr. Ransom had demanded to be released and checked himself out against the doctor's orders." The nurse gave Laurel a sympathetic look. With a final check of the monitors, she left.

Alone now, Laurel didn't bother fighting the tears.

Sometime later—she must have slept again— Jake and Shelley showed up, arms laden with a huge teddy bear whose face bore a comic expression, and a box of chocolates.

Before she could thank them, Jake said, "The DNA results came, sis."

It took a moment for her to process the words. "Sis? Like as in I'm your sister and you're my brother?"

"Just like."

"We always knew, you and I," Shelley said to Laurel, then sent a smug glance in Jake's direction.

Tears filled her eyes, tears of joy and gratitude this time. "That's the most wonderful news I've ever heard."

"We think so, too," Shelley said.

"How long have I been here?"

"Going on two days," Jake said.

Two days? Had it really been that long? Laurel tried to sit up, forgetting that she was tethered to a bunch of tubes connecting her to machines.

Gently, Shelley eased her back down. "You were out of it, sis. Did you forget that you were shot? Twice."

"I've been shot before."

"I'm sure you have. Doesn't change the fact that getting shot knocks the stuffing right out of you."

Memories of the time in the Collective's camp pushed through the lingering fog of the last two days. "What happened to Jenni-Grace?"

"She's in the county jail, awaiting trial," Shelley said. "Seems she's been doing some talking."

"Bragging's more like it," Jake said. "According to one of my buddies, who's a US Marshal, once she started talking, she couldn't stop. Turns out that she was behind Ronnie's arrest. She told the authorities where to find the evidence against him. She wanted him behind bars so she could take over. She was planning an accident for him in the not-too-distant future. He'd served his purpose, and she didn't need him anymore.

"Turns out that she's used the accident ploy before to get rid of people who were in her way, including her parents."

"Her parents?"

Jake nodded. "She arranged for their boat to explode. She had an iron-clad alibi when the explosion occurred, so no one looked at her. The lady has a string of murders to account for."

Shelley perched on the bed, careful of the tubes attached to monitors. "She can't hurt you anymore, so put her out of your mind for now. We want you to come to work for us."

"For S&J?"

"The very one."

"Is this a pity job because I can't be a Ranger anymore?" Laurel asked. No one had said anything, but she knew. Maybe she'd always known, but this latest injury to her shoulder had sealed it.

"Now that's just stupid," Jake said. "We want you because you're a great operative. You're smart, gutsy and don't back down even when the odds are stacked against you."

"Say yes," Shelley implored. "S&J needs you.

We need you." She gestured to Jake, who stood at her side. "Tommy's already talking about seeing his 'Aunt Laurel.'"

"Shelley's right," Jake seconded. "We do need you. As an operative. And as our little sister. Somebody has to look out for you. We sort of thought Mace would be here and that you and he—"

Exasperation shone in Shelley's eyes, and a taut silence stretched between the brother and two sisters. Laurel understood. They'd thought Mace would be around and he and she would look out for each other.

"He hurt you," Jake said, mouth folding into a hard line.

"Hey, it's okay," she said, pushing out a smile to defuse Jake's anger. "Mace and I are friends. He has no obligation to me, and I have no claim on him. So we're good." She was proud of the fact that she was able to get the words out without breaking down and crying like she wanted to.

"The doctor said we could spring you in another couple of days," Shelley said. "I'm bringing you home with me. And I don't want to hear another word about it."

"Okay." The idea of spending time with Shelley's beautiful family was too appealing to reject.

"Caleb and I won't take no for an answer. You deserve some pampering and spoiling, so don't go arguing... What did you say?"

"I said, 'Okay.'" Laurel discovered she wanted to hang around in Atlanta, at least for a while. Whether or not she took the job at S&J was another matter. It was a dream job, except for Mace.

And even if Mace wanted to be with her, she wasn't sure she could picture a future for the two of them. She'd told herself that she'd never again become involved with a soldier after Jeffrey. He had been her first love, but his ego hadn't been able to withstand the idea that she had made the Rangers and he hadn't.

And though Mace had left the Rangers, he was still a soldier at heart.

He would always put his life on the line, with causes to champion, victims to help, justice to serve. It was who he was, and she wouldn't change him for the world. She loved that about him. She also feared it. They had come close, too close, to losing their lives.

In the next instant, she knew she was lying, if only to herself. She'd take Mace just as he was. And why was she even debating this with herself?

Her elation over the news about the DNA tests took a backseat to the acceptance that she had no future with Mace. He'd made it clear with his absence that whatever they had shared was over.

TWENTY

After staying away from the hospital for a day and a half, Mace knew what he had to do. He didn't know if Laurel would see him or give him his walking papers. Maybe she'd see him for a minute only to kick him out. He deserved that and more.

She'd taken two bullets for him, even knowing that it would likely end any dream of continuing her career with the Rangers.

Unbearable guilt had caused him to walk out of her room and out of her life, but he'd discovered something. He couldn't stay away. If she told him she never wanted to see him again, that would be that.

But he had to try.

He urged Sammy, who had been staying with him the last twenty-four hours, into the truck and headed to the hospital. He'd need backup in facing Laurel. She might turn him away, but she'd never turn away Sammy.

Using a dog as his wingman would be down-right funny if it weren't so cowardly. He thought of Laurel's fearlessness and was shamed by his own lack of courage.

After explaining to a hospital official that Sammy was a service dog—and, really, wasn't that the truth?—Mace and Sammy took the elevator to the second floor.

He hadn't expected to run into Shelley and Jake as he walked down the corridor to Laurel's room.

"What's got you looking like you're trying to walk forward but your pants are on backward?" The words were delivered without a trace of humor as Jake blocked Mace's way.

Intent on his mission, Mace had no time for whatever bug was crawling up his friend's butt. In addition, a crowded hospital hallway wasn't the place to get into this. With Jake's aggressive attitude, the two of them were more likely to be trading blows than words.

He pushed his boss aside.

Jake pushed back. "I told you not to hurt Laurel. You ignored me. Now I have to pound on you." He made to raise his fist as though intending to follow through on it there in the middle of the hospital.

Mace took a breath. Held it. When he slowly expelled it, he knew what he had to say. "I'm on my way to make it right. You can pound on me some other time, but I've got to see Laurel. You try to stop me and we're going to have trouble."

Apparently sensing the tension, Sammy gave a sharp bark, as though to say "Play nice."

Shelley placed a hand on her brother's arm. "I think he means it." Though her tone was conciliatory, the look she aimed Mace's way was anything but. "You fix what you did to Laurel, or you'll answer to me."

Given his choice between taking on Jake or Shelley, he'd take Jake every time. A mama grizzly looked mild compared to Shelley when it came to protecting family. An ex-cop and former Secret Service agent, she'd bragged more than once that she could take down a man using only a pen.

"Look, I know I messed up with Laurel. I stayed away because I thought she couldn't forgive me for what happened."

"Did you shoot her?" Shelley asked in her practical, no-nonsense manner.

Taken aback, Mace stuttered, "Of c-course not."

"Then why would she need to forgive you?"

"Her shoulder…she'll never be able to go back to the Rangers now."

"The Rangers are pretty great—no question there, but they're not the only way Laurel can use her skills." Shelley grinned. "It so happens that I know of a security/protection business that just offered her a job. She hasn't said yes yet, probably because of a man whose brain is all wrapped up in some misplaced guilt."

"Laurel will be working for S&J?"

"If she takes the job. As soon as she's recovered enough, we hope she'll be our newest operative." Shelley bent to pet Sammy. "And Sammy, too, of course."

Mace wanted to whoop with joy until he remembered what had brought him to the hospital in the first place. He needed to make things right with Laurel. If he didn't... He didn't finish the thought. He couldn't.

"That's great. Now, if you'll excuse me, I've got some begging to do."

None too gently, Jake clapped him on the back. "Groveling helps."

Mace knew that Jake had had to do some serious groveling to convince his wife, Dani, to marry him, and, for the first time in a couple of days, smiled and meant it. "So I hear."

Laurel pushed a button that raised the bed setting a couple of notches and reached for the box of chocolates. After reading the legend, she chose a chocolate cream. With her first bite, she gave a moan of pleasure. Kale may be healthy, but chocolate beat it every time.

The idea of working for S&J filled her with excitement as well as a new sense of purpose.

She welcomed the challenge of helping people in trouble. And working alongside Shelley and Jake was just about perfect.

The broken pieces of her life were falling into place. Broken pieces. Broken people. She thought of the calligraphy piece in Mace's home. Yes, she was broken, but that didn't mean she was beaten.

With a determined swipe of her hand, she brushed away the tears that had been her constant companion since she'd learned that Mace had left. Though he had rejected her, she knew that the Lord would never turn His back on her. With Him on her side, she would find a way to go on.

She would stand strong in broken places. She had made herself who she was, who the Lord wanted her to be. Nothing could take that away from her. Nothing would.

With her faith to root her, she took a hard look at herself.

There'd been a change in her over the last week, an acceptance of her past and of her future. She'd made peace with both, as well as with her feelings about Bernice, and had even discovered she could feel a measure of grace for the woman and for herself.

If only Mace could find the same acceptance. He would have to come to that peace in his own way, in his own time. She prayed he'd find it.

He deserved that, deserved to be happy. She'd

have given anything if she could help him on that journey, but it wasn't to be.

A knock at the door had her looking up. And he was there. With Sammy. Bewilderment and pain swallowed her.

Mace did something she never thought she'd see from him. He shuffled his feet. Actually shuffled them. Like a small boy who'd been caught in a misdeed and didn't know how he was going to get out of it. "I brought Sammy. Thought you might let me in if he was with me."

Hearing his name, Sammy trotted over and nudged her hand.

Awkward with the IV drip attached to her arm, she patted Sammy's head. What kind of foolishness was Mace talking about? "Why wouldn't I let you in?"

"Your shoulder."

"What does that have to do with it?" she asked, honestly bewildered.

"You can't return to the Rangers. You'll have to resign."

So that was it. "And you think I blame you. You're an idiot, Ransom. A total idiot."

"Yeah?"

"Yeah."

"If you hadn't taken those bullets…"

"If I hadn't taken the bullets, my shoulder would have still been injured. And my career with the Rangers would have still been over. I think I've known it all along. I just didn't want to face it."

"All the therapy—"

"Was to help me hold on to my dream for a while longer." Laurel reached for his hand. "You helped me in ways I can never repay. But I'm good. And I'm ready to move on with my life." She paused. "Shelley and Jake offered me a job with S&J. I'm tempted to say yes, but…"

"But what?"

"Us." She refused to give in to the temptation to duck her head and instead met his gaze unflinchingly.

"Us?"

"You and me. We'd probably have to work together on occasion. Can you handle it?"

"I can handle anything with you at my side." He paused. "You and the Lord."

"I *did* hear you praying," she said in wonder. "The first night I was here. I thought I'd imagined it, but it was real."

"It was real all right. So was the prayer I said when you were shot, begging the Lord to spare your life. I thought I'd have a hard time getting the words out. Turns out it wasn't hard at all. I thought the Lord hadn't heard me, but I was wrong."

He pressed his lips to hers. "Now I'm begging again. Begging you to forgive me. I don't deserve that any more than I deserved the Lord's forgiveness, but there it is."

"I've been thinking a lot about grace in the last twenty-four hours. God gives grace to everyone, even those who don't deserve it. Especially to those who don't deserve it, like myself. If He can do that for me, then I should be able to extend the same to you."

"You mean it?"

"With all my heart."

"I love you, Laurel Landry. I think I've loved you from the day we met when I saw you take on a goon who outweighed you by a hundred or more pounds. I love you," he said again. "I always will."

Unlike many moments of pure truth, this one was not fleeting. Feelings ebbed and flowed, until Laurel was so filled that she thought she might burst from the joy of it. *Thank You, Lord.*

After kissing her again, Mace straightened. "You are my world. My heart and soul. Before you, I was floundering my way through life, trying to find a reason for my existence. I didn't know which way I was going or even why I was going there. You gave that to me. That and so much more. Marry me and make a life with me."

Nothing could have been more right. A ball of emotion pushed up from her heart to settle in her throat.

"Yes. I want a life with you," she said. "A big, noisy life that makes sense of what we do."

Gently, he took her hand in his. She looked at their linked hands. Both were strong, capable hands, nicked and scarred by the work they'd chosen.

She saw love and so much more in his eyes. She saw a future. One they could share. Tears, sweet and warm, came then.

With exquisite gentleness, Mace reached out to thumb them away, then laid his lips upon hers. They, too, were sweet and warm.

"I love you," he said again. "In case you didn't hear it the first time. I love you."

"It took you long enough," she said, despite the huskiness of her voice which was thick with yet more tears.

He grinned. "That's my Laurel."

"And, by the way, I love you back."

He had shown her a side of herself she hadn't known existed: a side that not only wanted but needed the love a man like him could bring to her world.

"You are my world," he said. "The sun, the moon, the stars. If I lost you, nothing else would matter."

Unspeakably touched, she pressed her palm against his cheek. "And you are mine." The brush of his lips upon hers promised everything she'd ever wanted. "Thank you."

"For what?"

"For making me the happiest woman in the world."

"Thank you for saving me."

One corner of her mouth quirked into a quick smile. "We saved each other. And the Lord saved both of us."

"We'll make a life together. A good one. Children. Sammy. And love enough to last a lifetime."

"And eternity," she added.

"And eternity." He took her hand and kissed the center of her palm. "I can't promise that we'll never have any problems, but I can promise to always be there to count the stars for you."

* * * * *

If you enjoyed Inherited Threat, *look for these other great books from author Jane M. Choate, available now:*

Keeping Watch
The Littlest Witness
Shattered Secrets
High-Risk Investigation

Find more great reads at www.LoveInspired.com

Dear Reader,

I hope you enjoyed reading Laurel and Mace's story. In many ways, this is also Sammy's story. With his missing leg, Sammy, like others of us, does not measure up to the world's standards of perfection.

The world's ideals of beauty and value, as evidenced by awards ceremonies, magazine covers and other superficial criteria, will never be the Lord's. He asks that we give of ourselves—of our hearts, our minds and our spirits—to serve others, for when we serve others, we are serving Him. When we do this with compassion, faith and love, we find favor in His eyes.

Missing legs or other physical imperfections matter not nearly so much as missing or unused hearts. I pray that we can each offer our hearts to the Lord, for He will turn our weaknesses to strengths, our flaws to honor, our sins to virtue.

With gratitude for His love,
Jane

Get 4 FREE REWARDS!

We'll send you 2 FREE Books plus 2 FREE Mystery Gifts.

Love Inspired® books feature contemporary inspirational romances with Christian characters facing the challenges of life and love.

FREE Value Over **$20**

Get 4 FREE REWARDS!

We'll send you 2 FREE Books plus 2 FREE Mystery Gifts.

Harlequin® Heartwarming™ Larger-Print books feature traditional values of home, family, community and—most of all—love.

FREE Value Over $20

BETTY NEELS COLLECTION!

Buy 3 and get 1 FREE!

Experience one of the most celebrated and beloved authors in romance! Betty Neels will delight you with her signature brand of storytelling: happy romances, memorable couples and timeless tales of lasting love. These classics have been combined in 2-in-1 books for your reading pleasure!

YES! Please send me the **Betty Neels Collection**. This collection begins with 4 books, 1 of which is FREE! Plus a FREE gift – an elegant simulated Pearl Necklace & Earring Set (approx. retail value of $13.99). I may either return the shipment and owe nothing or keep for the low members-only discount price of $17.97 U.S./$20.25 CDN plus $1.99 U.S./$2.99 CDN for shipping and handling per shipment.* If I decide to continue, I'll receive two more shipments, each about a month apart, each containing four more two-in-one books, one of which will be free, until I own the entire 12-book collection. Each shipment is mine to keep for the same members-only discount price plus shipping and handling. I understand that no purchase is required. I may keep the free book no matter what I decide.

☐ 275 HCN 4623   ☐ 475 HCN 4623

Name (please print)

Address   Apt. #

City   State/Province   Zip/Postal Code

Mail to the **Reader Service:**
IN U.S.A.: P.O. Box 1341, Buffalo, NY. 14240-8531
IN CANADA: P.O. Box 603, Fort Erie, Ontario L2A 5X3